CONFESSION

L/

LINNEA NILSSON

To Sarah
Thanks for being so
supportive of my writing.
Best wishes
Linnea
xxx

LINNEA NILSSON

A SKITTISH ENDEAVOURS BOOK:

Originally published in Great Britain by Skittish Endeavours 2023
Copyright © Linnea Nilsson 2023, All Rights Reserved
First Edition

Thanks to:-

Copy Editor: Dee Groocock of Stellar Reads

For more information on Linnea Nilsson see her Facebook Page at

https://www.facebook.com/LinneaNilsson

Book 1

CHAPTER 1

Panic!

Where have the men of old gone? I asked myself, after the umpteenth frustration and having finally disconnected from the dating site. I knew the answer: they had all grown old.

I had at least three accounts, one for every occasion. The sexy one, the more sentimental one, the mysterious one. But each time it was a disappointment.

It wasn't an easy life being single; especially being a high-profile, four-hundred-euro-an-hour lawyer. It was awe-inspiring, the men were frightened, they thought I was going to fleece them and, if someone suggested marriage, that I was going to leave them with their arse out in the cold.

In reality I didn't think about all these things, I just wanted to meet some handsome hunks, spend a cheerful night and then go our separate ways.

I'm not easy going, I'm high maintenance, I admit it, but I have my reasons. Receiving twenty to thirty messages a day, you'd think I'd have a good choice, but I didn't. Often they were from guys who wouldn't even stop to read what I had written in my profile. Just seeing a picture of a beautiful woman was enough for them to make their cognitive faculties go to hell. I had now classified them into categories and I knew how to recognise them immediately, right from the first line. One thing was certain, we wouldn't understand each other. I mean, would you send poetry to someone dressed in latex? The poems were often indecipherable, the kind that would require you to go through the Oxford Dictionary and still have work to do, as if you were interpreting Joyce's Finnegan's Wake. No, I wasn't even close to finding the right guy like that. And what was this fixation with cars anyway? I mean, after two minutes of chatting, someone would inevitably go on to describe their car. No, move on.

Then there were the dickheads ones, i.e. those who sent a picture of their penis. Without even deigning to say hello or show any courtesy. OK, in one of the profiles I had sexy pics, but from there to start chatting with a penis was a long way off. No thanks. If they had at least tried to write a couple of words. I didn't expect a novel, but two words written with the left hand were really too few.

Rarely did the kind soul take the time to describe himself; among the day's messages I finally found an intriguing one: nice, who had spent time reading me and even hinted at flirting and making a few jokes. It was a shame he had to be relegated to the un-fuckable group, because he was such a nice guy. How come after months of searching I still hadn't managed to find a fucking decent one?

Considering the cost of the membership fee to the various sites and the recent results, the return on my investment was definitely low; if nothing else the site kept me busy in my tired moments. It was almost five o'clock and I decided it was time to shut up shop and relax for the weekend.

I took one last look at the Ms Casati file, open on the table, and felt a moment of embarrassment. It was Friday night and time to cut out and prepare for a weekend once again as a single woman, but something was holding me up at my desk.

Ms Casati, an attractive brunette in her mid-forties, had recently inherited a fortune, real estate, various assets, and even a few companies in Switzerland since the death of her only parent, and Studio Martini and Associates was in charge of formalising the transaction. That would be me. Ms Casati was an old client, as the firm had handled her divorce case some three years earlier. A difficult situation; her husband was a bastard who had left her for his secretary and, not content with that, had insisted on making the case as difficult as possible for dear Ms Casati, out of sheer malice. As if she, unaware, had caused all that distress.

In the end, the poor woman earned a substantial income, an unspecified number of properties (one in Courmayeur, on which I was determined on principle to not let go, more than anything else), but above all, a lot of freedom from an odious husband.

The separation was quite tormented and the good Ms Casati decided to put an end to the opposite sex, forever. From what I had heard, she was now living with an attractive redhead, a former model and seven years younger; they had recently married in Canada and seemed a happy couple. I hadn't dared ask for more details; even though I was dying of curiosity, especially to find out how they had met, what had changed so drastically in her life to make her decide on homosexuality, but I had always restrained myself from asking. At the end of the day, one had to try to maintain an adequate professional level. I had to admit, however, that Ms Casati looked ten years younger and was unrecognisable compared to the woman I had met in the past, devastated by a terrible divorce.

Even the way she dressed had changed, certainly more studied; in a way sexy but not vulgar.

It wasn't the first time I had met divorced women who then turned their attention to the same sex, and at least three other clients of the firm had done the same although, I had to admit, Ms Casati was by far the most interesting case.

Eventually I closed the file and the computer, put everything in my bag and headed home. Shit, it was probably going to be a weekend spent trying to get laid without being fooled at the same time.

The last guy I'd met the week before had looked promising: attractive, well-dressed, confident, only to turn out to be a total bore in bed. I would have had a religious career ahead of me after all those missionaries.

After dinner I lay on the bed to review Ms Casati's file, after all she was paying me a lot of money for that inheritance and I wanted a job well done. My colleague Giovanni, a true Stakhanovist who spent more time in the office than anywhere else, would have been proud of me if he had known, but I wouldn't have given him the satisfaction.

It was around eleven o'clock in the evening when, exhausted, I put the files back in my bag. I needed a distraction, but reconnecting to FindApartner.com was not an option. Those messages would have sent me into a depression and that was not allowed, at least not on a Friday night.

I thought back to Ms Casati and how, despite all the troubles she had endured during her divorce, she had managed to land on her feet, with an exceptionally beautiful partner, tailor-made for her. What could have made her change her mind so much as to consider a woman as a partner? Tired and sleepy, I decided to explore the matter further during one of the following days. It was bedtime, I had made an appointment for the next day with a young man I had found online, and to show up with bags under my eyes would not have made a good impression.

CHAPTER 2

I took my mobile phone out of the bag and looked for messages. A text from Federica inviting me for that evening to go to a new trendy club they had opened, not far from Corso Como.

- What time?

- I'll pick you up around nine.

- OK.

- Dress smart.

Strange, I thought there was only one disco and a lot of places to dine but nothing else in the Corso Como area, maybe I was a little behind. Federica arrived on time as usual and we set off in the direction of the club.

"Tonight is going to be a bit special, I'm warning you."

"As long as it's not boring. I need a man, a real one, I'm taking one rip-off after another," I said.

"I was thinking about it, after what you told me about your last date. I've been scrambling to get this invite."

"An invitation-only club? How does that work?" I asked curiously.

"I don't know exactly either, I just know that a

friend of a friend is part of this group. They move around all the time and there's almost no way of knowing where the party will be next. They rent a venue and the next time they go to another place. Just think, they even bring their own waiters so that nothing leaks out."

"And what exactly did this friend of yours say is going on?"

"He didn't tell me a damn thing, I had to get the words out of his mouth with pliers, even though he was half drunk. All he said was that you have to dress up and expect to witness spicy things. He sent me a code on my mobile phone so I could get in."

I just hoped it wasn't one of those lame little shows where they were doing stripteases, although it sounded weird having to show a code at the door. Curiosity was piqued.

We parked near the theatre and before getting out Federica handed me a carnival mask. Mine was scarlet and covered the upper part of the face, leaving only the tip of the nose and the mouth uncovered. It was finely decorated and had red-grey feathers on one side and lace on the other. It was an expensive and stiff mask that had probably cost a lot of money. I watched in amazement as she put on hers, which was gold. It too had decorations on the face, glitter all around the bottom and a beautiful multi-coloured flower on the left side.

"Where did these come from?"

"They're part of the entrance fee. I had a hard time finding them, it's not like it's carnival time. Oh, rule number one: never take off your mask."

"Are there any others?"

"Wait..." she said, taking the mobile phone from her bag. "Here: never ask for names or exchange personal details. Never talk about what goes on in the club outside the club."

"What is it, *Fight club*? Rules already broken by your friend," I added.

"Indeed."

I put on my mask and we walked towards the address. It was a yellow nineteenth-century building but it wasn't really a club, it looked like the entrance to a house. At the front door were two burly men who would not have looked out of place in the NFL, whose stern faces kept the onlookers away. A couple in front of us, also masked, were entering.

"Can you show me the invitation?" asked the taller of the two. Federica showed the code on her mobile phone and the two stepped aside to let us in.

"First floor." said the same guy casually.

We looked at each other's faces and once through

the barrier we laughed like crazy, knowing that somehow we were committing fraud. We shouldn't have been there in the first place. We exchanged a look of complicity and started to climb the stairs, not knowing what to expect. Another energetic man, this time in a mask, asked to see our pass again and then let us into the huge apartment. There were well-dressed men and women, we could see multicoloured masks coming and going. The ladies had beautiful dresses, I noticed a few from a couple of designers I was following. I grabbed two glasses of champagne from a waiter who walked past us and then addressed my friend.

"So, what now?"

"We look around. I'm a bit disappointed, all I see is people talking, whereas I was expecting a rave party."

Federica took me by the arm and we started to walk around the immense and elegantly decorated living room. It was my friend who elbowed me, drawing my attention to a couple on a sofa far away, almost covered from view by several people. The woman was half-naked and kneeling, wearing only thigh-highs and high heels, and a mask. The man was sitting on the sofa and... I couldn't believe it. The woman was performing oral sex on him, there in front of everyone, to general indifference. A man wearing a Casanova mask approached, lightly caressed the woman's hips and then moved on.

Federica and I looked at each other for a moment.

"That sounds less boring than I expected."

"What do we do now?"

"We walk around like we're regulars and what happens, happens," I said.

Federica was approached by a young man who looked good, despite the mask, tall and dark and with two deep dark eyes.

"Are you new?" he asked directly.

"No, it's not our first time," lied my friend.

"Can I get you something to drink?" the man said, motioning Federica to follow him in the direction of the little bar that had been set up in a corner of the living room. My friend looked at me and I shrugged, as if to say, that's why we're here. She smiled at me and started following the hunk.

I wandered around the living room, trying to get a grasp on what was going on. Most of them seemed to know each other, but I began to notice other people who, like me, were wandering around in isolation, looking around. I left and headed down the corridor where more large rooms were waiting for me. I opened a door and saw a group of four people, two women and two men, watching another masked couple making love. I continued further. This time I arrived in a second living room, smaller than the previous one. Here, too, people were talking and then, on a nearby sofa, two naked women were kissing each other eagerly. One looked younger, with long, curly, copper-red hair, the other in her forties, very fit, with short brown hair. The latter was lying on her back as the redhead kissed and caressed her from above. It seemed... wait a second... I was stunned and motionless. Could it be that... those two reminded me very closely of Ms Casati and her new companion? Could it be that that elegant, sweet lady was the same one I was looking at? She was wearing a diamond ring and I tried desperately to recollect if I hadn't seen it before, but I couldn't remember.

It was at that point that a man in his thirties approached me.

"It always has that effect to people who are being introduced for the first time," he told me almost in a whisper.

I turned around sharply. It was another light mask, from which I could guess a very attractive face, belonging to a guy in his thirties, with green eyes and very black, curly hair. He had a strong jaw, a one day stubble and an intoxicating perfume. He was taller than me, despite my heels, and for a moment I was tempted to ask the identity of the two women. I barely restrained myself, remembering the rules.

"I'm not easily surprised," I said, "but this is actually the first time."

The man grabbed my hand and walked towards the bar, almost dragging me with him. He offered me a glass of champagne, which I swallowed in one breath and then handed me another. I turned to look at the two women making love and my unknown companion noticed it.

"We can get closer if you want."

I nodded in agreement and he took me under his arm. We made our way to an armchair set a couple of feet away from the two and the man sat down. "Here, get on top of me," he said, tapping a hand on his thighs. I took another sip and sat down on top of the man who now had his hand on my hips. The two women continued to make love and now the redhead was kissing what I was increasingly convinced was Ms Casati between her legs. Around them there were other couples interested in the scene and some dared to caress themselves in front of the two. I was getting excited and so was my guest: I could feel his erection under me, it was getting bigger and throbbing regularly. I settled down to better feel it. I took another sip and put the glass on the floor, then leaned with both hands on the arms of the chair. While I was entranced by the scene of the two of them, I levered my arms over the armrests to rub myself against the sex of the individual beneath me. He was big and I would have liked to isolate myself with him, but from what I understood that was not an easy option in that place.

The stranger put down his glass and started caressing my legs. I cursed my friend Federica for not being more specific. I was wearing a tight, dark grey office suit that didn't allow for much movement. I would have to make do.

The man began to rummage under my jacket and unbutton my blouse. He had strong, sure hands that knew what they were doing. A shiver ran down my spine as they passed lightly over my breasts. He would surely have felt my hardened nipples.

I had had sex with perfect strangers before, but this was beyond anything I had experienced before. I was wondering what my friend Federica was doing. Those hands were creeping under my blouse, caressing my hips and then going up again. He was undoing my bra and I immediately felt the warmth of his strong hands on my chest. I was rubbing myself against his sex and soon we began to have our own audience. I could still see the two women, about whom I was hypnotised but now other people appeared around us. A thin blonde woman stood in front of me and took off my jacket, placing it to the side, on the floor. Then she lifted my chin and kissed me. She had two full, sensual lips and her tongue was entwined with mine. Then, as if nothing had happened, she left.

The stranger below me had exposed my breasts completely and was now caressing my legs from behind. We were attracting a lot of attention from the neighbours, a man on the right was stroking his crotch while on the left was a couple: the woman was in front and the man who, from behind, had started stroking and undressing her. I looked around and it seemed as if the time for chatting was over and many people were getting busy undressing. One woman grabbed me under the armpits making me stand up and slowly unzipped my skirt, sliding it across the floor, and then stepped back, heading towards her partner. I sat back down on top of my handsome stranger who in the meantime had pulled down his trousers. I felt him hard against me, prodding me with his erect member and grabbing my breasts. I stood up again, this time on my own initiative and turned around. I climbed on top of him and we began to kiss. His hands slipped under my panties and caressed my bottom. I removed his tie and began to unbutton his shirt, feeling his pectoral muscles under my fingers. He was in good shape, he probably spent a lot of time at the gym because he had very defined abs. My hands ran over his firm, dry chest as he pushed against me, his member still trapped under his boxers. We kissed for what seemed like an infinite amount of time, continuing to tease each other, but I wasn't going to last very long. I was as wet as ever and I wanted him inside me, I didn't give a damn about the people around us watching, if nothing else they were helping to make me even more aroused.

I moved away, kneeling in front of him. I took off his boxers, exposing his hard, gnarled member, ready for mating. I kissed him, first on the tip of his penis and then slowly moving down to the base. I continued to tease him with my tongue until I felt someone from behind pull down my panties. I turned around and saw a not very tall brunette kneeling behind me, intent on removing the last of my clothes. She slid my panties down to my knees and then invited me to lift my legs up, one by one holding my thighs and pulled them off, letting them fall back onto the pile of my clothes, then helped me take off my blouse and bra. I resumed kissing the stranger's member as the woman probed my hips and clawed at my bottom. I rose to position myself on top of my partner and he penetrated me, his member sliding into me without difficulty from how wet I was. He lifted me up with those strong arms of his and let me fall back on top of him, I could feel him pulsing inside me as the woman from behind helped him, going along with his movements. She held me under the armpits making me rise and fall as if I were a puppet in her hands and I felt her rubbing herself against me. Her large breasts brushed my neck, increasing my cravings; I was gripped by this stranger who was fucking me relentlessly, aided by a woman I had never seen before and surrounded by people watching or making love to each other. By now no one had any restraint and nor I with them. I moved faster, throwing myself against the man and trying to find the right rhythm. Our flesh slammed into each other, the man filling me completely with that hard rod as I felt hands reaching for me, definitely from the brunette. She stroked my back, then took my nipples between her fingers; sometimes she took me by the neck forcing me to kiss her. I was in a state of unprecedented excitement, I no longer cared who was doing what or with whom. I was only focused on my own pleasure. I sped up and was almost on the verge of coming when suddenly I decided to turn around, I wanted to feel him enjoying himself inside me while watching those two women on the couch. I stopped the contact, turned around and let the man take me from behind. I resumed my rhythm and now I had the brunette in front of me blocking my view.

I pulled her to me and kissed her, then grabbed her by the hips. I had her against me while the stranger continued to pump me from underneath and I held on to her, my chin on her shoulder so that I could see for the last time those two women, maybe Ms Casati, who were making love to each other on the sofa in front of us. The orgasm took me suddenly and I embraced the stranger even more fiercely. I didn't want her to pull away or block my view and I held her against me. Our breasts rubbed together as my sex throbbed with orgasm, but it wasn't over yet. The woman's and the stranger's hands were working in sync, commanding me, lifting me up so I could fall back on that huge rod. It was shortly after that the man came out of me and came, making a moan and slumping down in the chair. I sat back down on top of him, now satiated as the woman continued to caress me.

The two women on the couch got up and went into another room, out of my sight.

I got up shortly afterwards, gave my handsome stranger a long kiss of thanks for giving me one of the best orgasms in recent times and stood up. I looked at the woman who had assisted me and kissed her too, then grabbed my clothes and headed for the door. For some mysterious reason I didn't feel the urge to cover myself, I walked in just my thigh-highs, a mask and a pair of stilettos, keeping my clothes under my arm. I was possessed, I was desperately looking for the two women when I entered one of the rooms and recognised Federica's mask. She was naked and struggling with two men, one was taking her from behind while holding the other in her mouth. I smiled at the scene but didn't feel I should disturb her. I continued to wander through the rooms and finally made my way to the bathroom. There were naked and clothed women going in and out or tidying themselves up. I did my business and went in front of a sink to freshen up for a moment and it was at that point that the redhead came out of a cubicle. I looked at her fixedly in the reflection of the mirror and then looked around again for her companion whom I didn't see. While I was distracted the redhead came after me, also naked, and pushed me against the sink, pressing herself against me. She caressed my breasts and then put her hand on my neck, pushing me further towards the mirror and making me bend over. Then with her other hand she caressed my legs, slowly moving up to my sex. She lapped at my clitoris in a circular motion and then moved on to feel my bottom. She smiled at me and went back to feeling my sex, then she lowered herself and I felt her tongue beating on my vagina. She gave me a quick kiss between my legs and walked away leaving me there half aroused. God what was happening to me? Could it really be the Ms Casati girl? I cursed myself for not paying attention, I could have watched her better, tried to look into her eyes. What colour were they, damn it?

I was lost in thought when the brunette who had been busy with me and the stranger entered the bathroom. She didn't waste any time and came towards me and when she was right in front of me she kissed me again. She too touched my hot sex and then slipped a finger inside. She started to masturbate me there, while other women were washing their hands or fixing their hair. She pumped me with one finger, rubbing her thumb against my clit. She lifted my leg and held it up so that she could penetrate me better. That double contact was driving me crazy, she had guessed my rhythm and kept on fucking me like that non-stop. I held her close, kissed her neck and then those full lips again as she worked her way between my thighs. By now I was delirious, at that point of excitement I just wanted to come one more time. The orgasm was coming again and stronger than ever as she stroked my swollen sex. She almost brought me to the point of coming and when she saw that I couldn't take it anymore, that I was rubbing myself against her without restraint, she lowered herself and began to lick me. It didn't take long for me to feel the contact of that skilful tongue and the fury of pleasure took me. I leaned against the sink and pushed her head against my sex. She drank my juices, she sucked me, she penetrated me with her hard, wicked tongue. And then I exploded. I felt the orgasm take over my sex and continue up my stomach and make all the hairs on my body stand up. I let her drink in my juices until she was satisfied, then she lifted herself up and said, "You taste good."

She took a business card she kept in her thigh-highs and slipped it into my hand. "This is for the next party. Don't miss it."

And then she turned and walked out as if nothing had happened, disappearing into the crowd.

I was exhausted, with wobbly legs and completely satisfied. I leaned against the wall for a moment, trying to regain my strength, and then I went out again. How much time had passed? It seemed like an eternity.

I looked around trying to spot the redhead without success and then I bumped into my unknown companion.

"I'll see you again." he said with a half-smile, "How's that for a first date?"

I didn't answer, grabbed him by the arm and led him towards one of the sofas that were still free. We made love again, this time without interruption.

Then I gathered my clothes and went to look for my friend, hoping that she had also finished for the evening.

Federica joined me, fully dressed, a few minutes later at the entrance. It had been several hours since we had entered.

"How did it go?" she asked with a mischievous smile.

"I think I've lost control a bit. I need a drink," I told her straightforwardly. I had always been in control of the situation, in my work life and also in my private life, including in matters of sex. But this time I had really let myself go and it was scary.

"You look like you've seen a ghost," said my friend.

"In a way."

"Come on, let's go for a drink, these people give me the impression they want to go on all night and I'm already half wasted. A beer and some fresh air will do us good."

We left the building and headed for one of the local bars. Federica hid the two masks in her handbag.

CHAPTER 3

I always thought about myself as bisexual, but I never fully explored that side, apart from the occasional one-night stand. I thought I was born like that, but I never really acted upon it. Too much pressure from society, despite living in Milan. Did I really want to explore that side of me? I knew I wouldn't like to keep it in the closet if that was the case, I would not go out with friends or for a business dinner presenting my partner as "a friend". People weren't really tolerant when it was a matter of sexuality, despite living in a large city, where it was supposed to be on the edge of modernity, not in the Middle Ages. The catholic mentality didn't help one bit. What a circus! Eighty percent of the catholic priests were gay and the church was the most homophobic institution we had in this country. Ms Casati's choice intrigued me. Of course, our situations were different, she could do whatever she pleased from her mega villa and with all her money. It would make her appear even more glamorous, but me? I had clients; I could not afford to lose some of them even if I could; I had a mortgage to pay. As soon as I formulated that thought I realised I was bullshitting myself; it was none of their business. People would switch lawyer on a whim anyway, because they got up in the morning on the wrong foot, because a competitor was lowering the price, because a friend of a friend recommended someone else. I would lose customers no matter what and I would gain others. I was just lying to myself trying to find justifications.

And so I went back to my usual dating site.

As I was about to log in, an idea came to me: when registering, the site asked for sexual preferences, so I decided to change tactics. Registering on the site cost a lot of money so the risk of meeting time wasters would be minimised. I went to the settings and changed my preferences to "men and women" and presented myself to the virtual world as a new, attractive, bisexual.

What now? I thought. Wait or come forward?

I tried to connect to the chat, but after about ten minutes spent reading other people's posts I found nothing that could give me an explanation, a glimmer of information on who I was. They all knew each other and talked about their own business and it was almost a shame to disturb them, and then what could I say?

Maybe I needed a chat room for lesbian novices

but I couldn't find any; and then how to overcome that block that always got me every time I entered a chat room? At first I was always on the defensive unless I spotted someone really attractive, but in an all-women chat room? I was lost.

I decided to look at a few profiles, mostly lingering on the photos; the site offered the possibility of finding an affinity partner so I clicked on the button, just out of curiosity, to see what would happen.

The first person was a fairly attractive blonde from Milan who worked in a shop in the city centre. Well-groomed but the description seemed a bit vague, only two lines.

The second person was faceless, I could only see a body in a bikini and, from what I read, looking for exciting moments and nights of passion. I continued.

The third person had no photo, lived in Dublin (Dublin? That site certainly had some imagination, how can you associate Milan and Dublin?) and the profile was definitely intriguing. StrangerDanger, as she had decided to call herself, was an actress of about twenty-six who lived in Dublin, practiced judo and was American. As I read her description I discovered that she was sometimes mistaken for Italian (maybe that's the connection), Japanese, French and someone had even apparently asked her (seriously!) if she was black. A short self-description and at the end the invitation: if you are not scared yet, send me a message.

Why not? I thought. After all, she was in Dublin and an email wouldn't cost anything, at least I'd get to practice with my English.

I wrote a short message and, after a couple of seconds of hesitation, pressed send. It's done, I said to myself.

I closed the computer and let myself be taken into the arms of Morpheus.

CHAPTER 4

The following Monday I asked Giovanni for advice, because some aspects of the Ms Casati file did not sit well with me.

"Giovanni, would you have a moment to discuss Ms Casati's will? There are some financial aspects I don't understand," I said as I appeared at the door of his office, smiling as brightly as I could despite my tiredness. Giovanni looked at his calendar for a moment.

"Yes, I'm free around ten, bring the file,' he replied. I wondered if he was thinking of billing me for the work, but I immediately regretted it, as Giovanni had always been a wonderful person, at least with me. And his financial knowledge was immense.

Once back in my office I couldn't contain my curiosity and logged into my personal inbox to see if I had received any messages in the meantime and found an email from someone called Patricia. I opened it and it was a reply to my weekend message to the Dublin chick.

She told me she was glad she hadn't scared me off with her profile, that she was currently stuck in Nebraska (where she lived) and had made a few friends in Italy and would soon be visiting the country as soon as she raised enough money. Patricia told me that she had worked in the theatre when she was in Dublin, it was not always easy to get a part, she very often found herself working part time in a pub or as a waitress in a restaurant. In her own words she dish washed her way through half of Europe.

In Nebraska, she worked for a local gym teaching fitness. The letter continued, telling me a little about her interests, some Italians she had met in the past and saying she had never visited my country.

In particular, she told me that she had met a gal called Simona in a hostel in Germany and found that she had many interests in common with her, including theatre. Simona had taken a year's holiday at the end of her studies to travel and live a carefree life before getting a steady job. They spent all day talking, and continued into the night, aided by a bottle of red wine. Before going to sleep, each in their own room, they made a pact: if they both felt the same attraction the next morning, when Simona was due to leave, they would meet in the living room of the hostel and go on together.

Patricia forgot to set her alarm clock and woke up at nine in the morning, an hour after her appointment with Simona. She ran in her pyjamas down the stairs but she was already gone.

They wrote to each other after a couple of days, but the moment had passed.

The letter went on to ask for some personal information, which I gladly answered, and I also added some unsolicited information.

I returned to Giovanni with a box full of documents and we sat around a table in his office (his desk was constantly flooded with paperwork) that was used mostly with clients.

"I remember Ms Casati, a divorce case, if I'm not mistaken," he said, running a hand through his grey hair, as if to help himself remember.

"Yes, this time, however, it's about her father's death, which left her with nothing less than an insurance company, several corporations, and a few scattered accounts, including two in Switzerland."

"What do you want me to do?" he asked, as usual direct and without wasting any time.

"Actually, I'm not sure, which is why I thought you could help me. For example, I'm trying to trace who actually controls these accounts in Switzerland and one of the companies, Gerald Tore Capital Management. They receive funds from the insurance company, but I've been trying to trace back to the parent company and I'm lost, having followed the trail to Luxembourg, through the Caymans, the Isle of Man, Jersey and back. It doesn't seem to have any real parent company."

"Hmm... give me a couple of days to review the paperwork. Usually these Chinese boxes are used to hide a lot of dough for the purpose of evading taxes."

"Tax evasion?" I asked with immediate interest, after all Commendator Casati had never given me the impression of a person willing to engage in shady dealings. Not to mention his daughter, who was the kindest and most affable person I had ever met.

"Usually it's about moving funds from one place to another, often these are legitimate, if unethical, activities, but if you have to take an inventory of everything, you have to get to the bottom of it."

I pondered this for a moment and replied, "Ms Casati would like us to liquidate part of the properties and companies; she is certainly not interested in becoming an entrepreneur."

"Giovanni laughed and said, "With that piece of arse she has as a companion, I too would spend the rest of my life spending money and having fun."

"Don't be nasty, come on. If we're going to

liquidate the companies, we need to make sure we don't commit any fraud, and guarantee we don't get Ms Casati into trouble," I replied.

"OK, fine, fine, you don't have to lecture me. Like I said, give me a couple of days, and if I get stuck I have a friend who is a computer genius, for the right fee he can help me follow the flow of money."

I remembered his 'friend', we had used him on a previous case and it had cost us a fortune. Not that I could complain about the results, but the first time I met him I was extremely surprised. I thought I was looking at some geeky kid, a typical hacker in scruffy clothes, but it was actually a man with a moustache, in his mid-50s, working as a consultant for one of the biggest multinational computer companies in the world. This guy in a suit had been working on computers since he was in his early twenties and had accumulated an impressive background in computing. In addition, working mainly with banks and insurance companies as part of his 'official' job, he was always able to fish for information directly from the source, when he couldn't bypass security.

What a character, my colleague Giovanni, he always had unlikely people as friends.

CHAPTER 5

The days went by slowly and by now I had cancelled my accounts on the dating sites, I wasn't going to get anything out of them anyway. I took the invitation card the mysterious woman had left me out of my purse and turned it over in my fingers. There wasn't much written on it: it said to send a message to a telephone number quoting a code. I did it, but nothing happened. Discos, bars, hangouts, I had already ruled out using my friendships to introduce myself to someone, despite my desire of having sex. I had already had a go at the nice ones but I doubted that I would have gone beyond a second date.

I was left with chatting to Patricia, which had become a daily occurrence. She'd even sent me a picture, allowing me to put a face to all those words. God, how much she wrote.

She had long black hair and a stunning smile. I could see why she had been mistaken for an Italian; there was something familiar about her face. She was 5'7" and kept herself fit. She was certainly a beauty, but she was totally different from what I had imagined. I was expecting a typical blonde from California, but instead I found myself writing daily to this girl almost ten years younger and sometimes even flirting with her. She had sensitivity, the girl, even though she often hid it behind her well-shaped and firm body. She had even sent me a photo of her dancing from behind, showing a firm, well-defined bottom, narrow hips and smooth calves ending in thin ankles.

It was that day that the surprise came.

"I have enough money to go on a new tour of Europe and Italy has always intrigued me. I'm in contact with an Irish pub in Milan that would even take me as a waitress. I'm studying Italian, but I'm not really very good at it even though it's a lot like Spanish. The only problematic thing is the accommodation. I wouldn't know where to start. Would you put me up for some time? At worst I'll go back to Dublin."

I was stunned. Host her? She didn't even know me. We had exchanged phone numbers and sometimes flirted on WhatsApp, but it was a long way from hosting her at my place. What if she was a psychopath? What if I disliked her or she started bringing people home?

I kept looking for excuses to say no, but in my heart I knew I wouldn't find any. Nothing we had said to each other gave the impression of anything wrong, on the contrary, she had always seemed like a nice, level-headed girl. I had money, if things went south I'd put her up in a hotel or on a train to Ireland, why not take a chance?

"That's fine with me," I replied, "when are you going to show up around here? In the meantime I'll send you the address, you already have my number."

"Is next week too soon? That pub job won't be available for long."

Fuck! Next week? I thought. I was panicking, maybe I should have shut down the communication and disappeared, like so many people do on the web, but I was excited and intrigued. Patricia could still be a good friend, I kept telling myself, even though a lot of alarm bells were starting to ring in my head.

"Perfect. Let me know your flight and I'll pick you up at the airport."

We continued to chat for a while but the damage was done. My mind began to wander - which room would I put her up in? What would happen to my privacy if I wanted to bring someone home? What if she did?

We would set the rules on a case-by-case basis, there was no need to worry too much at that point. I would have asked her opinion about Ms Casati anyway, if only to find out more about my client. I knew it was a morbid curiosity, which had nothing to do with the firm or the work I was doing, but by now I was hooked.

CHAPTER 6

I found Ms Casati and her companion in my office the next day. They didn't have an appointment, but with the amount of hours we were billing her, they wouldn't need one.

"Linnea, dearest," she said as she came in. I stood up and went to shake her hand but instead she hugged me warmly as if I were an old friend. The redhead behind her nodded her head in greeting.

"Please, have a seat."

They sat down in the armchairs opposite my desk, "Can I offer you something to drink?" I asked them.

"A couple of coffees would be fine, my dear." The companion agreed without a word.

I instructed my secretary to take care of it and headed for Giovanni's office. "So, is there any news?"

"News about what?" he asked me as if he were falling from the clouds.

"On the Ms Casati file, they're in my office," I hurried.

"The redhead too? Hell, you could have let me know, I would have brought you the files myself just to lay my eyes on that hottie."

"Giovanni!" I rebuked him, "be professional. So, those papers?"

He handed me a container and then added, "the short version is that we can release the liquid funds, about twenty million or so. They're in one of our transfer accounts, the details are in the file. As for the real estate, apart from a couple of buildings downtown all the others are under the control of the insurance company of which we still know little. That one we still have to investigate, so all those assets remain under administration. I'm doing my best to speed things up but there's a lot of paperwork."

"Don't worry about that, just keep digging."

I picked up the pile of papers and went back to my office. The two of them were having a conversation but stopped as soon as I entered the room. I took the papers that were on top of the pile and started studying them.

"We can currently release nineteen million seven hundred and fifty thousand euro. Transferable today to an account of your choice." I said.

The women nodded, then Ms Casati resumed, "What about the remaining assets?"

"For those we'll have to wait a little longer. The insurance company, well, there are complications there. We've found a few anomalies, a series of Chinese boxes of parent and subsidiary companies scattered halfway around the world, and until we have proof that it's all legal, we can't release them."

"Would it be worth talking to the insurance company's legal department? I'm sure they can clear up any doubts." Not a question that required an answer, the redhead opened her purse and handed me a business card.

I set it aside and continued, "Then there are some properties we can transfer. All it takes is one signature today on these papers and everything is set. Here," I said, looking at another sheet of paper, "This building in Corso Vercelli and this one..." my blood froze in my veins as I recognised the address, "this one in Corso Como." I handed the papers to the elegant lady who signed them without hesitation. I was astonished, that was the same building where I had gone with Federica. I tried to look at the two women, trying to figure out if they were the same ones I had seen making love on that couch, but nothing leaked out. I had been so surprised and excited that night that I had forgotten every detail. The redhead had the same hair, but seeing her in front of me at that moment, I couldn't be sure. She was certainly a beauty, and Giovanni was right to drool over her. She was at least six feet tall, with two pronounced breasts, skin as clear as the moon and two breath-taking legs. She was wearing a long Cavalli dress, which made me a little envious; Ms Casati, on the other hand, was more classic in a dark blue dress. There was no sign that they recognised me, although the redhead could well have been the one who kissed me between my legs in the toilets of that building on Corso Como.

"Well, here are the details of my account," Ms Casati said, handing me another sheet of paper and the newly signed papers. "We'll talk again soon, I'm sure."

Having said that, the two of them stood up and said goodbye and then headed for the door. I watched them walk away, still trying to figure out if they were the two I had seen. Damn, I'd never have known.

CHAPTER 7

I was in Malpensa waiting for Patricia's flight to arrive; I would have to keep an eye on the one from New York as there was no direct flight from Nebraska. I felt like a little girl at the fair, although there was no good reason for such excitement. We had flirted online a few times but I kept telling myself not to get my hopes up, we didn't really know each other and she might even dislike me.

I saw her come out of the baggage claim area about twenty minutes later, beautiful as the sun and with a radiant, infectious smile. Her trolley was packed to the brim with luggage and she had even brought along a saxophone. Or at least that's what it looked like from the case. She was dressed casually while I was dressed up even though it was Saturday. It didn't suit me but I wanted to look good. I waved and she headed in my direction. We spoke in English.

"Welcome to Italy," I said without preamble, though it sounded a bit corny, and then we kissed on the cheeks.

"I'm dead tired, luckily they didn't lose any luggage."

"I thought you were staying for a few months, not moving house," I said nodding at the mountain of suitcases.

"I like to travel light. Seriously when I move I want to have my own little world at my fingertips, my own stuff. I can't really afford to buy clothes or do any other shopping so I take everything with me."

"Including a saxophone?"

"Including that, I've been studying for a couple of years."

We arrived at the car and it took quite a while to load everything in the Land Rover, some of the suitcases ended up in the back seat. Luckily I didn't have a sports car. Patricia seemed to be in a coma from the journey and spent most of the time dozing, she wasn't company but I was fine with that.

When we got to my flat I showed her to her room and made her a quick plate of pasta, just to make her feel at home but instead she seemed almost embarrassed at the disturbance.

"Not at all, pasta takes about ten minutes to make."

"Do you know if there is any theatre where they play in English?" she asked at one point.

"Not that I know of. We are multicultural but not to that extent. At most you find a few cinemas that run films in the original language, but not much else. You told me you also sing, I know of friends who sometimes supplement their evenings by going to play in the Navigli, maybe that's a possibility, apart from the pub."

"I'd like to see some of these clubs, just to get an idea of what the air is like."

"If you want to take a nap in the afternoon, maybe you're fresh for this evening and we can wander around a bit."

"That's all I ask for, my own personal tour guide."

"Something like that."

CHAPTER 8

I still wasn't used to living with a stranger, I felt like I was a student again, and perhaps bringing Patricia into the house hadn't been the best idea. We got on well and she was a really nice person but I hadn't yet gone so far as to ask her about her sexuality and, more importantly, about that Ms. Casati doubt that was plaguing me.

I certainly couldn't interview her during dinner, or could I? That was one thing I hadn't done yet, take her out to dinner. It would certainly have helped to break the ice between us. I had bought her flowers a few days earlier. We had talked about it online some time before, and she once told me that she had never received flowers in her life. It seemed to me to be a serious failing on the part of the rest of humanity so, once in the office I organised an Interflora, heading to the pub where she worked in the afternoon. I couldn't remember the last time I'd bought flowers myself, nor how much I'd had to spend. Too little and I would have looked like an imbecile: the first time you get flowers and a skimpy bunch arrives? No, I wasn't going to do that. I thought a hundred euro would do the trick and gave the details to the shop, which flowers to choose and so on. In the card I wrote "With the wish of a dazzling career in cinema and, at worst, as the best dish washer in Europe. Kisses. Linnea."

It was a surprise when I saw her return with a bouquet of flowers of stratospheric proportions. I had embarrassed her and felt like a jerk, she almost had tears in her eyes.

"I couldn't believe it when they arrived," she told me. "The delivery man said 'Patricia' and I said yes that was me, but I didn't realise the flowers were for me. The others looked at me dumbfounded wondering who they came from and I didn't know. I hadn't found the card." She said in one breath. "Everyone who came in looked at the flowers and asked questions I didn't have an answer to. Then I found it when I picked them up to take them home. Now they all think I'm a hottie, getting flowers from strangers." she laughed.

Then she put the huge bouquet down on the table and threw her arms around my neck, giving me a kiss on the cheek, followed by a whispered "thank you".

"Come on, I'll take you out to dinner," I told her to cut through the awkwardness that had set in.

"First flowers and now a date? I'm flattered." She

said teasing me and creating further embarrassment, this time on my side.

"Put like that it doesn't sound good, I sound like a stalker, but... but yeah, let's just call it a date."

"Sold. Where are you taking me, to one of those little candlelit dinner places? You're going to put my virtues in jeopardy." she said in a set voice, as if she were in the theatre.

"We'll see. Just don't make me look bad."

"Then I have to dress up. Just elegant or sexy too?"

Baloney, she was cornering me; my fault for flirting and now I was stranded, struggling to stand up to her. It wouldn't have happened with a man for sure, but Patricia had something disarming about her, she could put me at ease even when she was clearly taking the piss.

"Suit yourself, wear whatever you think is most appropriate."

She shrugged and headed for her room, coming back out a few minutes later in an understated, elegant black suit. She spun around and then asked, "Is this OK?"

"Perfect."

We dined like old friends in a French restaurant downtown. No candlelight.

CHAPTER 9

I had arranged a meeting with the insurance company's law firm for that week and was going over some notes Giovanni had passed on to me when a message arrived. It was very similar to the one Federica had received, a code, an address and the basic rules. The eagerness to find a man had worn off a little over the previous weeks but I had found that evening extremely intriguing. I was undecided. I would have liked to participate at least once more in one of those wild orgies but something was bothering me. A thought crossed my mind, how was I going to explain this to Patricia?

Then I shook my head as if to banish it, without succeeding. There was nothing between the two of us, nothing that could even begin to compare to a relationship, or even the hint of one. We were friends and that was enough, but I was still troubled by the thought of how she would judge me if she knew. What if she'd taken her luggage and left? I found it hard to admit it to myself, but her presence reassured me, despite the age difference. I was comfortable, it was like being in a happy relationship without being in a relationship. I didn't know how to justify it anymore and maybe I was really attracted to this woman.

I took out my mobile phone and sent a message to Federica: "Do you still have those carnival masks?"

"Yes, why?" came the reply, punctual.

"We have another invitation."

"But how... When? ... I mean, do you want to go?"

"Not alone. This Saturday."

"Count on it! Last time it was A-OK!"

I sent her the address and we agreed that I would pick her up on Saturday late afternoon, we would have a light dinner in Monza and then head to the address. A villa in the Brianza hills.

I rented a car that time, since we were going to a private house and I wanted to safeguard our privacy. When we arrived at our destination, we stopped in front of a gate where two men stood guard. We had stopped earlier to put on our masks and as usual they checked the invitation on my mobile phone. I could see, from where I stood, several luxury cars already parked in the courtyard in front of the villa. It was a huge two-storey building probably built in the eighteenth century and a driveway led to an area near the house where there was a huge garage and a clearing for cars. There were at least thirty of them, but after us I saw a couple of limousines drive in and unload several couples. My rented Volvo didn't stand out among the other cars.

When we entered we were immediately attracted by the stucco and the good taste of the house, old but sober and not too heavy. As usual, there were other people in elegant dresses like the previous time, but there was also a different, more tense atmosphere.

We entered the main hall and I saw a different scene from the one we had witnessed before. Surrounded by guests was a lady dressed in leather and a completely naked man on all fours with a collar around his neck. The woman was walking him around like a well-trained little dog without him batting an eyelid or protesting.

Federica looked at me in amazement and I shrugged, we were on the floor now and we were going to dance. We looked around and immediately noticed other particular situations; it was clearly an evening of domination and submission and we were not at all prepared on the subject. We took a glass of champagne and casually approached a small group who were talking, trying to get some tips.

A tall man was explaining to other guests about his 'slave', a well-dressed blonde who was sitting on the floor, hugging his leg in adoration.

"One thing the dominant partner must keep in mind is: train, train, train," the man said with authority.

"Every training has a purpose, you have to order, show and make the slave obey, even if this sometimes involves unpleasant activities. Here, for example, my slave is striking a pose of respect and waiting until I order her otherwise. Humiliation above all, has the highest goal in the training of a slave. This forces the submissive to make the right decision to obey his Master and be subject to his will."

"So the slave becomes for all intents and purposes a property to be used?" I intervened. Federica's face turned red, what little I could see of it, and she elbowed me. She was trying to remind me that we were not part of this circle and a low profile would certainly help in going unnoticed. I ignored her.

The man looked at me for a moment with deep eyes, as if a teacher had finally met a brilliant pupil, and added, "exactly! You force her to realise how profound this decision is and how obedience is not always easy." Some people around nodded.

"It's like with a puppy dog. Or a bitch, in this case," I said referring to the little blonde squatting at his feet, "humiliation becomes a tool for instruction."

"Exactly, my dear."

Then the man went on to describe some of the practices of humiliation and I felt Federica drag me away by the arm.

"Have you gone soft? Do you want to give us away?"

"Come on relax. We're all masked, who cares about two random chicks. Surely they don't all know each other, we might as well be legitimately invited."

"Okay, okay, but don't get too exposed, all right? Otherwise there goes the party."

"Sure. How about we split up? I'll meet you in the lobby around one o'clock and if either of us feel like leaving early, we'll take it upon ourself to go find the other."

"Agreed. There were a couple of muscle guys buzzing around me last time, maybe I'll find them again."

"Happy hunting," I said, and she walked away without a word. I continued to listen to the man for a few minutes until I was convinced that, all things considered, I had figured out how I was going to behave for the evening. I had the ground rules, now I just had to find someone to put them into practice.

I started to go around the rooms and at one point I saw a guy on all fours with his hands and feet tied up, the owner was giving a demonstration of obedience and inviting the guests to command without restraint. A grey-haired man took off his shoes and ordered the slave to lick his feet. The slave promptly obeyed. Then the mistress invited the others to do the same and a queue of people formed, waiting for their turn. A lady threw some food on the floor and the man prepared to lick it. A third lady was heavily insulting him when another individual, much older than average squatted down next to the victim and started to masturbate him. My turn soon came but I could think of nothing; I looked around and saw a riding crop left unattended on a table and hit the slave on the buttocks with it. A resounding roar filled the room and for a moment I thought I had gone too far, but instead I received nods of approval and the abuse of the others grew higher. A woman straddled the dominated and carried herself around the room, hitting the unfortunate occasionally, as one does with a horse at the races.

I decided not to let go of the whip; even though I was intrigued, I had no intention of being mistaken for a slave by some unknown person. Better to make things clear from the start.

I wandered around the premises until I laid eyes on a young man in his mid-twenties who seemed quite lost so I decided to approach him.

"Slave or master?" I asked, banging the riding crop in my hands.

"Slave, but I belong to that woman over there." he said showing a slightly chubby lady who was explaining her views on domination to a couple of couples.

"Great."

I got closer and when there was a pause in the conversation I approached the dominatrix and asked, pointing to the young man "I was wondering if I could get some practice with your property."

"Help yourself, a bit of training will certainly do him good."

I thanked her and turned back to the guy who had meanwhile stood at attention.

"On your knees, you have been ordered to obey me."

"Yes ma'am."

I turned around him as if to decide what was going to happen next even though I had no idea. Doubts assailed me, how was I supposed to act? Would they notice that I didn't know anything about those things? Maybe I should have just jumped in and seen how things went.

"Follow me."

The man came after me on all fours until we reached an armchair, where I sat down. I saw the mistress glance at me from time to time, but she didn't seem worried or jealous so I continued.

"Take off my shoes and lick my feet."

The young man bent down in front of me and took my foot, very gently. I looked around and saw that other guests were undressing or playing sex games so I relaxed, the important thing from what I understood from the previous time was not to be the first to do something, otherwise I would have captured an audience.

It took him forever to get my shoe off and luckily I wasn't wearing stockings that night, then he kissed my big toe. He took it in his mouth and started sucking on it and when he was satisfied he moved on to lick the sole of my foot. That feeling of power, of having the possibility of absolute control over the situation was turning me on, not to mention the young man at my feet who looked decidedly attractive.

"Get undressed, slave!" I said at one point. The man obeyed and stood up. "Slowly, don't rush things or you will be severely punished!"

"Of course, my lady."

He was actually quite a looker, he had two firm buttocks and outlined pecs, sculpted abs and strong, muscular arms. When he finished, I made him kneel again and probed the hardness of his flesh with the riding crop. He was in good shape.

"Make your mistress come, lick me!" I said spreading my thighs in front of the man. This time I had been more careful and had avoided wearing a tight skirt; there was the problem of taking my knickers off but I wanted to see how he would cope.

He approached me further and put his head between my thighs, sniffing my juices. Then he very gently began to pull off my panties and kiss me on my sex. He knew how to do it, he licked dutifully and in the right places while I was half lying on the armchair; every now and then I gave him a little tap with the riding crop when he went too far away from my clitoris, just to keep him in line. I was wet, I really wanted to feel him inside me, but the slave boy was passive, not taking any initiative without a specific order.

"Perhaps Mistress wishes to sit on my face?" he asked at one point.

I hadn't thought about it, I was so immersed in being licked that I had completely forgotten about my dominant role.

"Lie down on the floor!"

The man obeyed and I went to position myself on top of him, then squatted down. I was literally sitting on his face and for a moment I thought I was going to suffocate him, but he kept licking me. I saw his erect penis and started stroking it with the riding crop. This gave him a shiver. I could feel it between my legs, that tongue was creeping into me and the way I was sitting, with every movement his nose was rubbing my anus, giving me further cause for excitement. I began to masturbate him, feeling him hard and strong between my fingers. I stroked his cock, I could do anything and the man would not say a word. I rubbed it, took it in my mouth and when I felt that he was experiencing pleasure I stopped. That was the game, to be able to handle that sublime body at will. I kept teasing him and then letting him go. I was almost close to an orgasm myself, so I got up and sat down in the armchair.

"Fuck your mistress!" I ordered him, "And make her come."

The man came on top of me and I finally felt him inside me. He had grabbed my thighs and was pumping me like a madman, in and out non-stop. I could hear him panting against me, his hips pushing that gnarled stick until it filled me, then emptying and starting again.

I grabbed him by the hips and pushed him against me, I was close, I was going to cum. I was furious, I was thrashing around, I had my legs wrapped around him to feel him better, he was throbbing and quivering with every moan and... and then the orgasm came hard and sudden. My sex throbbed with pleasure as my wetness poured against it; I cried out.

Then I relaxed for a moment as he continued to pump me. I pushed him away by pressing my arms against his chest and then pushed him away again by kicking my foot against his body. He was frustrated, I could clearly see him in front of me, his member standing upright with desire, the urge to finish and cum in my body was clear on his quivering face. But that was none of my business, let him go to his mistress and, if she was in a good mood, give her the reward she deserved. I gathered up my panties, which I placed in my handbag, and left.

CHAPTER 10

I kept going round the rooms and at a certain point I saw the redhead. She was on a sofa and sitting at her feet was the woman I was sure I had identified as Ms Casati.

The redhead was ignoring her and continuing to talk to her friends so I kept my distance and watched them. I ate a canapé and grabbed a glass of champagne while I studied the situation. Should I have gone to the redhead and asked permission? I was hesitant, surely they would recognise my voice and I wanted to avoid that. It seemed that silence, bellowing and grunting aside, was the rule at these parties so I decided that would not be the case. I was about to attack a second glass of champagne when the redhead and her friends left, leaving Ms Casati alone, naked and kneeling by the sofa. This was my chance. I approached stealthily and when I was behind her I put my hand on the back of her head. She made a movement with her head to see who I was but I didn't let her, not completely. I wanted her to know I was a woman, but that was all. I pushed her against the couch and she obeyed by getting down on all fours. "Good bitch," I whispered, then stroked her ample bottom. She tried to look around, perhaps to see if the redhead was watching or at least giving approval. She seemed lost.

With one hand I had her pinned by the nape of her neck to the sofa while with the other I probed her flesh, squeezed her firm bottom, her full and quivering thighs. She was undecided whether to let me do it, perhaps in doubt about disobeying her mistress, or to let herself go. I touched her sex with my fingers, which I then licked. It tasted good. I ran a finger against her sex again and sought out her clit, which I began to stimulate and pinch.

"Wait, don't..." she tried to say.

"If you disobey, your mistress will punish you severely!" I told her. It wasn't true but I tried my luck and that seemed to calm her down. I lifted my skirt and began to rub myself against her from behind, by now I had lost all restraint and wanted to enjoy that firm, ripe flesh. She moaned.

I felt her clitoris harden under my strokes and after several manipulations of her sex and caresses on her breasts she finally seemed to be properly wet. I got her up and kissed her on the mouth, our tongues intertwined and I felt her warm, full lips against mine. It was when we parted that she recognised me and her mouth opened wide in surprise. She looked around again for a way out but I didn't let her. I took her by the arm and dragged her out of the room into an adjacent corridor. No one paid any attention to the two of us on this evening of orders and obedience. With some reluctance she followed me to a room that was strangely empty. I pushed her onto the bed and locked the door behind me.

She was lying on the bed waiting so I hurriedly took off my clothes and got on top of her. We kissed greedily while I explored her wet sex with one hand, making her moan with pleasure. She had firm breasts that I began to kiss, her nipples were hardened and exposed to my tongue teasing them. She had a beautiful, curvy body that responded to my every touch. I turned her on her stomach and brushed her anus with my thumb, while I penetrated her with my index and middle fingers. She vibrated against my hands, her humours lubricating my fingers allowing me to go deeper. Ms Casati moved her hips back and forth, moaning with every stroke I gave her. The idea of being in an unfamiliar house while I was fucking a client had made me wet beyond belief, I wanted to enjoy it on her face, to feel her shudder beneath me. I didn't worry at that point about what might happen next, in that moment I was gripped by pure lust and it seemed my partner was doing the same.

"Don't stop, I'm close." she said moaning but it was at that point that I stopped rubbing her. I spun her around again, this time with her back against the mattress and grabbed her leg, forcing her to encircle me like that. Our sexes were in contact and I had started to fuck her, sex against sex, clitoris against clitoris. She was passive and relaxed as I towered over her. We held each other by the legs trying to increase the pressure against our sexes which were now throbbing with desire. I removed her mask and for a moment she was stunned, then closed her eyes and continued to move her hips until I felt her come. She clawed at my legs, quivering, thrashing wildly against my sex which was also on the verge of exploding, but I didn't want to come yet. When her orgasm waned, I took off my mask in turn and went on top of her, kissing her again, full of invigorated passion. Then I went on top of her and pressed my sex against her full lips. She indulged me and began to lick me greedily, I held her head by the nape of her neck and pushed her against me, giving her the right rhythm. She licked, I felt her tongue thrashing around inside me at times making me gasp. My humours were running down her mouth, making her face shiny, not long now. I felt my sex pounding and then an explosion of pleasure took over my whole body making me tremble with pleasure. I couldn't hold back and screamed out that immense orgasm and then slowly relaxed. I turned her over on her stomach and she obeyed without a word. I caressed her sex and then her ample white bottom, which quivered with every touch. She was firm and smooth but it was time to leave before the redhead found out and made a mess of me. I kissed her neck, ran my finger over her wet sex one last time and then lightly stroked her anus. I thought for a moment that I could penetrate her and I was sure she would let me, but I decided not to try my luck any further. What a pity I didn't have the whole night at my disposal and the aid of some vibrators. I hastily dressed and put my mask back on before going to find my friend.

Federica was puffing near the entrance, "Where have you been? I've been looking for you for half an hour."

"I was busy," I reposed smiling, "how did it go?"

"A deadly bore, what a drag all this business about slaves and masters. If only one of them had wanted to fuck me properly."

"Shall we go, then?" I asked.

"With both feet."

I took one last look around the room and saw the redhead talking to one of the bodyguards. It was time to skedaddle.

CHAPTER 11

Over the next few days I didn't get any visits from Ms Casati and her partner, but I did get an appointment from the insurance company we were investigating for that afternoon.

I had Giovanni bring me the papers, put them in my leather bag and set off down the streets of the city centre.

I was to meet the legal representative of the insurance company, a certain Giorgio Comaschi.

The office was near Piazzale Cordusio, in a nineteenth-century building, the entrance was all marble and stucco, with the aim of intimidating anyone who ventured into the office. I let myself be announced and a secretary collected me a few minutes later.

She looked familiar but I couldn't remember where I had met her before. I didn't pay much attention until I was in the presence of lawyer Comaschi. He was a dark-haired, well-dressed man.

"Are there any hiccups in releasing the shares to Countess Casati?"

Countess? That information had never been received, so my client was a noblewoman? It fit.

"There are irregularities, especially with these foreign parent companies, this one in Jersey and this one in the Caymans," I said, showing a document to my interlocutor.

The man turned red and then, in a firm voice, said, "You will do what you have been ordered to do, which is to conclude the paperwork for the inheritance. These things are not your responsibility!"

It was at that point that I recognised him. He was the guy I had first met at that party and made love to. Then everything became clear to me. I looked outside the glass door at the secretary. She was definitely the one who had given me the number for the second party.

"As I said, you will do as you are told," the man continued, "and if you don't like it, these will change your mind." He took some photos from a desk drawer and threw them on the table in my direction. They were photos of me and Ms Casati making love. Someone had certainly put cameras in those rooms, perhaps with the very purpose of catching influential people red-handed and blackmailing them.

"Can you imagine the headlines? Milanese lawyer involved in an orgy ring. The newspapers would be full of it for weeks and she would be completely smeared. We have influential friends in publishing, I assure you that if we were to get involved we could get you into a lot of trouble."

"Do what you think, this meeting is over."

I took my papers and left, slamming the door. I needed to talk to someone, but who could I tell this story to? Certainly not my colleague Giovanni and Federica would not have understood my doubts. Instead of going back to the office I decided to go home and think about it after a shower. Patricia was at home that day and had mentioned that she wanted to go back to Dublin and when she thanked me again for my hospitality I asked her if she would like to hear my story.

"Bastards!" she said when I'd finished, and then added, "but there is one thing I don't understand."

"And that is?"

"From the way you described this Countess Casati to me, she didn't give me the impression of a conspirator."

"What do you mean?" I pressed her.

"Well, she came out of a difficult marriage, you told me. My guess is she fell into the wrong hands. Maybe it's the redhead who's in cahoots with the insurance company and once she gets her inheritance, who knows what happens. Ms Casati looks more like a victim of a conspiracy than an accomplice. They've kept her out of it with this whole party thing, the pretty redhead who's wringing her hands day and night so she doesn't think about business."

"I'll think about it," I said, "When did you decide to leave?"

"Tomorrow. A friend is picking me up and the idea is to drive up to France and then take a ferry. It'll be fun."

"You've been a good friend, Patricia."

"You too, how can I ever thank you?"

"Well, when you're famous, send me tickets to a premiere."

"You got it."

And so I retired to my study to think. There was some truth to what Patricia had said, so I opened the computer and started writing a letter to the public prosecutor's office. I was going to denounce all the shenanigans I had encountered, especially with regard to the insurance, taking great care not to involve the Countess Casati. I had no evidence that she was involved and, above all, I was convinced by Patricia's version, that maybe she was just a victim.

I sent everything the same day.

A month later, the news of the arrest of Comaschi and several other accomplices appeared on the evening news. Among the accessories they showed the face of a red-haired, very attractive woman. No mention of Ms Casati. No mention in the following days of my spicy photos in the newspapers, maybe I had escaped.

I was in the office looking at the latest news when Giovanni came into the room and said, "Ms Casati is here to see you."

"Show her in." I readjusted my skirt and put on my glasses, as if to create a defensive barrier between us. Countess Casati entered in all her splendour and handed me a huge bouquet of flowers, then kissed me on the lips.

Perhaps I could have pursued my research into how Ms Casati had decided to become a lesbian directly with her.

******

Book 2

CHAPTER 1

I had picked him up in a disco bar. It hadn't been easy, the women were buzzing around him like flies on honey and it would have taken a stick to chase them away. But a man has his needs and when he went off to get a beer, the girls preferred to exchange opinions and look at his bottom instead of accompanying him. Big mistake.

By the time they noticed the problem and saw me it was already too late, by then I was standing next to this tall curly haired man who looked like a demigod and I had already put my hand in his trouser pocket. At that point the competition was out of the picture, I literally had him in the palm of my hand and I wasn't going to let him go.

He managed to mumble a few words but I wasn't really listening. I was captivated by the broad, muscular chest that was peeking out from under his shirt and what my hands were probing. If he had something important to say, now was not the time. I caught his name, Carlo, because he insisted on introducing himself but the only thing I was interested in was taking him home and taking his clothes off. He was at least ten centimetres taller than me despite my high heels and for once I thought I had won the lottery. That's how I liked them, no fuss when one grabs you by the penis and drags you out of a club on a Saturday night.

We took his car and I gave him the general direction, Carlo took off like a bolt of lightning and as soon as he had his seatbelt on I started massaging his member from above his trousers. I could feel it hardening and for a moment I even thought about taking it out. A beast like that should not be kept in a cage, it should be shown to the world as a trophy to be proud of. I changed my mind a few moments later when he almost lost control of the car.

"Keep your eyes on the road and don't get us killed," I told him, "I still have plans for the evening."

He nodded and resumed driving in the direction of the Navigli, where I lived. He had slowed down and I with him, now I was stroking him very slowly, but still I slipped my hand inside the zip. It was long and pointed upwards, one of my favourites. It filled my hand completely and was hard and erect; had it not been for the near miss a few minutes earlier, I would have wanted to taste it. There was time, I told myself, don't rush.

Carlo moved his hips and levered his back against the seat to help me in that contact, I caressed him going up and down and felt him vibrating in my hands. There was no apparent defect, it looked like a nice dick, one of those that fill you up and hit you just right. I just hoped it was one that would last, you never know beforehand.

"Here, turn right and then take the second right," I ordered. He obeyed without a word, his face was getting red and I was already feeling wet, waiting for the night to follow. "Stop, my flat is there, that door on the left."

He parked as best he could, quickly tidied himself up, although his penis remained visibly erect from under his trousers, and followed me.

We kissed in the lift and I started to unbutton his shirt, my hands running against his hairy chest, he kissed me on the neck and grabbed my bottom, squeezing it. I hurriedly opened the door as Carlo made me feel his sex from behind, we entered and I dragged him towards the bedroom. We looked at each other for a moment and then I pushed him onto the bed, where he let himself fall. I took off my skirt, remaining in my garter belt, and slipped off my blouse. I had some new black underwear, bought in the hope of a fiery encounter and for the moment everything seemed to be going according to my expectations. I climbed on top of him and opened his shirt completely and started kissing his chest. The hardness of his member was extraordinary, I could feel him pushing himself against me, and I had already decided that I would take the initiative. I unzipped his trousers and pulled them off, he let me. Then I climbed on top of him again and caressed his arms, strong and muscular, pushing them towards the headboard. I had a tie on the bedside table and with my left hand I grabbed it, passing it around his wrists. He didn't notice me doing this, he was too intent on rubbing his penis against my sex, and then I tied it to the headboard. When he noticed it I saw a moment of astonishment, but then he smiled at me so I went further. I took off his underpants and there he was in all his beauty, a dick raised upwards, the veins in evidence, and I knew he would make me feel all his masculinity, once inside me. I kissed it on the tip, making him tremble with pleasure, then I took it completely into my mouth, sucking him. He expressed his pleasure with a soft moan.

It was at that point that I got up and quickly went to the kitchen. I looked around and saw what I was looking for, a French kitchen knife, with a carved bone handle and a wide blade that faded slightly at the tip. I held it behind my back while I went back to the bedroom, where Carlo was waiting for me. I climbed on top of him again and showed him the knife, "Now I'm going to shave this beautiful hairy chest while you fuck me; don't make any sudden movements."

He looked at me with eyes full of terror and then began to look around, first to the right and then to the left, as if searching for an escape route. "Don't worry, I was only joking," I said, passing the back of the blade across his chest, "I would never allow myself to ruin this marvel."

It was when the back of the blade came close to his nipples that Carlo began to sob, "Don't hurt me, please," and he began to cry like a baby.

"Wait," I said, putting down the knife, "it was only a game." but by now Carlo's face was full of tears and terror, the cock that until a few minutes before stood erect against me had sagged like a balloon deprived of air.

"Let me go, please." he continued to cry and when I lifted myself from him he curled up in the foetal position continuing to whimper. I touched his penis and by now it was floppier than a squid. Fuck!

I sat down on the armchair next to the bed,

hoping he would recover, but after a few minutes the situation wasn't getting any better. I lit a cigarette, took the knife and cut the tie that held him prisoner with one swift blow. Carlo got up from the bed with impressive speed, gathered his clothes and ran out of the door, still naked.

Fuck, what a shitty night! I was going to have to use the vibrator for the rest of the evening.

CHAPTER 2

I arrived at the office earlier than usual and as usual Giovanni was already at work. "Did you spend the weekend here, within these walls?"

"No, don't worry, I had some paperwork to do for today and came in early."

Giovanni was a workaholic. He had started working in the law firm years ago with my father and then stayed on when I took over. Instead of retiring to the Riviera and going fishing like my parents had done, my dear colleague didn't want to relax. Not that I was complaining, he was a valuable partner and had endless legal knowledge, which proved useful in one of the city's most renowned law firms.

But sometimes I would have preferred him to take it more lightly, to take some of those damn holidays that kept piling up for once. I had understood the reason for this work frenzy years ago: it was due to the premature death of his wife in a car accident. Giovanni had devoted himself body and soul to his work in an unsuccessful attempt to forget.

The secretary brought me the mail and the list of appointments for that day and pointed out a new client, a certain Riccardo Liberati. It was a consultation for which I wouldn't have to prepare anything, which suited me fine since I hadn't fully woken up yet. I had a quick look through the mail and finally found a message from my friend Federica, asking me to call her back. URGENT! It said, underlined twice.

Federica answered on the third ring "hmmm, hello..."

"I saw the message, but are you still in bed?" I asked her.

"Hi Linnea. Oh that! Sorry I've had a hell of a weekend, I'm pissed off. Are there any of Ms Casati parties coming up?"

If only! I would have swapped my weekend for anyone else's, even hers. "Federica, it's Monday morning. If you have erotic desires on a Monday morning you need to get treatment!" and I along with her, as I hadn't been thinking about anything else since I had gotten up, but hypocrisy was one of my best weapons at the time.

"I need a nice strong coffee, and then you're right. I'll talk to you later in the week?"

"Count on it. Aren't you working today? Are you OK?" I asked her.

"I'm indisposed or at least that's the official excuse; I'm actually hungover as hell. If I get fired I'll ask my lawyer for help."

"Oh God, another pro bono. You'll ruin me."

We laughed and for a few minutes continued to tell each other about the most recent misadventures but I soon realised that Federica wasn't following me. She was probably already half asleep. I closed the communication and thought back to one of Ms Casati's masquerade parties, where sex was an integral part, usually themed.

Maybe that was the problem, sex permeated my life in all its aspects. I could be professional, I could behave like a 'normal' person most of the time and sometimes I could even be boring, but sex was always there.

Walking down the street, meeting customers and even in the supermarket I didn't see people, I only saw sex. A guy was buying oranges and I was looking at his backside, assessing its consistency, trying to see how firm it was to the touch, to see the shape covered by the jeans.

A client would walk into the office and without me noticing, my gaze would run to the crotch of his trousers, would it be long and knobby, bent up or straight? What would it feel like between my thighs? I didn't see men but pecs to caress, penises to suck, arms that would turn me inside out. And this happened with almost everyone and no one, apart from the unfuckables, they escaped my analysis. Every single day.

Obviously I wouldn't have made love to just anyone, but nevertheless the curiosity to see a naked body, to imagine what it would be like to make love to it, remained.

Even women were not immune to this treatment. As I walked around the centre I looked at them, I looked at their shoes and imagined we would be rolling around on a bed, kissing, caressing. I looked at their ankles; their calves were instruments that would surround my body, pushing me towards an open and wet sex, I studied the consistency of their thighs.

Women's legs under tight jeans that enhanced their solidity, skirts that rustled, highlighting their knees, which in my fantasies I caressed, feeling their roundness under my fingertips. I looked at blouses and saw breasts to kiss, some firm and prosperous, others soft and velvety, small breasts, nipples to stimulate with my tongue.

Every day I was on the lookout for someone I could take to bed, with an excuse, man or woman I was completely indifferent as long as they let me enjoy myself and play with their bodies. Strangely enough, I had never been with Federica although we had shared some experiences and I was intent on understanding the reasons for this when my secretary announced the arrival of Riccardo Liberati. My secretary; a great piece of arse with whom I had not even tried to flirt: that was a boundary I had set for myself long ago, never mix business and pleasure. I went to the meeting room where the new client was waiting for me, sipping coffee.

"Pleased to meet you, Linnea Martini," I said, offering my hand, which the man shook vigorously. He was a tall swarthy guy with an athletic build, a day-old stubble and a decidedly sexy appearance, but with two eyes that delved deep into the soul. Hard and direct that conveyed a feeling of danger.

"Pleased to meet you, Riccardo."

I sat down across from him and asked, "How can I help you?" The man began to sing the praises of Martini & Associati, how well known it was in the banking and insurance world, and gave a few names that had recommended us. They were important clients, so I decided I should pay close attention to this handsome man in a grey suit and dark blue tie with blue stripes. It was only when I picked up the notepad that I remembered that this was no ordinary tie. It was called an Old Etonian and was typically used by students who had attended Eton in England, another reason to listen to him despite the fact that another client would add to the workload.

Riccardo worked for a multinational corporation, a bank that dealt in investments all over the world, but his speciality was the US stock market. He had worked on Wall Street and had requested a transfer to Italy a few years ago. "I could be suspected of murder," he said at one point and that caught my attention.

"Who did you kill?" I said, keeping my eyes on my notebook and starting to take notes.

"No one."

"Maybe you should tell me your story from the beginning."

"That's probably the right thing to do," he agreed. He took a copy of the *Corriere della Sera* from his bag and handed it over. "This is the article about me," he said, pointing to a picture on the front page.

I took my time reading. A 24-year-old girl had been found strangled in her home near Porta Romana. The cops were investigating, following all sort of leads but nothing concrete so far. Liberati took it upon himself to fill in the blanks, probably seeing my doubtful face, by saying that they were lovers.

"No one knows that she was your girlfriend? Didn't you get a notice from the police? Hey, are you supposed to do it if you are under investigation?"

"She wasn't a girlfriend in the true sense of the word. We had, as it were, 'meetings'. I have a flat in the same building and we often did things."

"I see," I added while I didn't actually understand much of anything, but there would be time for explanations. "Why didn't you report to the police if you have nothing to hide?"

"Because of these," he took from the bag stowed near his feet a brown envelope and pushed it in my direction on the desk. I opened it and saw pictures of Liberati, naked as mother had made him, while strangling a girl, looking very much like the one in the paper.

"And you said you didn't kill anyone?" I asked again, incredulous.

"That's right. It's not what it looks like. We were doing some erotic practices, including one called 'erotic asphyxiation' but we never went any further. Someone took the trouble to photograph us and send me the images. As far as I remember the last time we did this was a couple of months ago." he said like a whipped puppy.

"So this is blackmail?"

"Most likely."

"Mr. Liberati, if I have to pry the information out of you, we're not going anywhere. If you want me as your lawyer, please spit it out and don't leave out any details." The man sighed and began to narrate.

He had met her by chance. Then he corrected himself and said that there were actually two girls, one named Luciana and the other Maria Sole. From their flat they could see directly into Riccardo's, which was at an angle to where they lived. At first, being spied on with the women he brought home was a source of excitement, just knowing that two beautiful girls were watching his every move was an uncontrollable stimulus. Then he got to know them and the erotic games with them began. They went on like this for weeks, each time pushing themselves slightly further until Luciana had said enough. She had found her own flat and for a while Riccardo continued to see Maria Sole.

"Which flat did you see each other in, yours or the girl's?"

"In mine, always. She shared hers with other students."

"So the police won't find any traces of your DNA in the flat. Anything else that might lead you back to Maria Sole, Mr. Liberati?" I asked.

"Please, call me Riccardo if it doesn't bother you."

"Fine. Go ahead." I wasn't extremely pleased with that new confidence with a potential client, but sometimes you have to suck it up.

"DNA I imagine there's plenty of in my flat and if whoever sent these photos decided to forward them to the investigators, I'd be in a real pickle."

"Why don't you come forward and state your whereabouts to the police? Where were you on the evening of the crime?" I looked briefly at the paper and added, "June 24th."

He didn't answer immediately and started looking out the window, or rather into the void. "I was with the other girl, Luciana."

Seeing me look up from my notes, he hastened to point out that Luciana was the one he actually cared about the most, which he had realised after she had left. They had spent the evening at a restaurant and the whole night together but Luciana had already decided to leave and spend her time travelling around Europe and perhaps South America. There was no way to track her down or know where she was. What's more, her relationship with the two of them had been kept in the utmost secrecy and so he had no knowledge of any friends or relatives to ask. There was nothing to say, Liberati was just in a lot of trouble, yet he wasn't giving me the impression of being a murderer, he was convincing me.

"Who would have an interest in taking those

photos and blackmailing you?"

"I've given it a lot of thought. I've ruled out all the possibilities and the only one left is chilling. The only people making money would be the people at the bank I work for."

"No ex-girlfriends, jealous husbands?" I pressed.

"That could always be the case but it seems unlikely to me that they would go that far. Instead the bank has a lot to lose. We're making a takeover and I've uncovered a lot of irregularities. You may have seen the news about Banca Popolare Fiorentina?" he asked and at my nod he continued, "We're at an advanced stage and I'm auditing the accounts. The bank in question has an SSO that..."

"What is an SSO?"

"An organised trading system," he hastened to clarify. I was aware of it. Instead of buying and selling shares on the market, a bank could appoint buyers and sellers within the bank itself, avoiding going to the stock market and paying commissions. I motioned for him to continue.

"I think, no, I'm convinced that they do arbitrage transactions, that is, they have the order they buy at less to sell at a higher price to the customer."

"I don't understand." Then Liberati explained to me that when faced with an order, for example, to sell shares by a client, the bank had to find a buyer on the market and vice versa in the case of a purchase. Instead of doing this, they used a brokerage firm that would go out and find the shares at lower prices (either on high internal markets of other banks or on the stock market) to sell them at a mark-up. These transactions were done in microseconds by high-powered computers and extremely fast connections. In effect, the brokers were beating the bank to the punch to find the best deal and getting in the way. This allowed brokers to trade risk-free, buying from one side and selling to the other within milliseconds, risking nothing. The client paid high prices while remaining in the dark about these transactions, the brokers got rich.

This brokerage firm, Liberati had discovered, had strong links with the top management of the bank, perhaps they were even in cahoots. When he reported the situation to his boss, the latter shrugged, and when he went over him to see his boss's boss, he was advised to let it go. When he went higher with his complaints, he was told in no uncertain terms not to meddle or there would be trouble. He was contemplating taking the news to a newspaper when the story of the murder came out.

I was wrong. Liberati wasn't in trouble, he was in muck up to his eyeballs.

"Give me the details of this Luciana and also of the superiors to whom you report to. I will make enquiries." Liberati began to write, "Oh, and I ask for ten thousand euros as a retainer and four hundred euros per hour, for my services."

"Pfiu! Wow, that's steep!"

"Riccardo, how old are you?" I asked in a rush.

"Thirty-four."

"Okay, imagine yourself at sixty-four, you just got out of *San Vittore* after thirty years spent among murderers and rapists who used you for a lifetime as their personal odalisque. In the meantime, you've caught AIDS and have an arsehole as wide as the St Bernard tunnel. But you've got a nice little nest egg saved up..."

"Message received, it looks like a sound investment to me. Do you take cheques?"

"We take everything, cash, cheques, Visa, MasterCard, PayPal. When you're done writing I suggest you take a nice holiday. Leave a number for emergencies but don't show up in the area, you can always say you didn't read the news."

"OK."

We said goodbye and I handed the cheque to my secretary.

CHAPTER 3

I went to Giovanni and told him the story of Riccardo, leaving him stunned. "But do you think this story about arbitraging is true?"

"Hell, yes! There have been some egregious cases in the United States." He told me about how some companies were doing their utmost to have their data centres as close as possible to the US stock exchanges in order to receive information with a few milliseconds' lead. It was enough to know in advance which orders had been placed and to exploit arbitrage between exchanges.

"Get me as much information as you can," he said, then headed for the door. I had to find that Luciana at all costs and I knew just the right kind of bloodhound for the purpose. I had a privileged relationship with the Pedrazzoli Investigation Agency and they would surely help me. If the price was reasonable. Their office was not far from mine and I would walk, although it was starting to get hot. Near the entrance of the building that housed the agency there was a street performer playing guitar and singing, but my attention was caught by her jeans. They were ripped, and the girl, a curly blonde with a stunning physique, was sitting on a makeshift stool. I could see that opening showing the pale, firm skin of her thighs and made me imagine how I could have knelt in front of her at that moment and caressed that golden skin. I imagined my fingertips lingering on her jeans and then slipping into that opening in search of her sex. I kept walking.

As I entered the building and the lift opened I felt two strong hands grabbing my arms from behind and push me inside against the wall. "Linnea Martini, you're under arrest for obstruction of justice and public indecency."

What? I thought about it for a moment and remembered several occasions when I had been guilty of both offences. The man added, "I have to search you."

Still holding me against the lift wall, the man grabbed my wrists and handcuffed them behind my back; I could not turn around. I felt him search my clothes and hips and then he lingered on my breasts longer than he should have. He took one of my nipples between his forefinger and thumb.

Then I felt him reach down and caress my legs, slowly moving up and feeling my thighs. "This search seems a little irregular," I said without turning around. The man continued down to my panties and then slipped a finger underneath. I could feel it on my sex as he searched me.

"Hmm... what do we have here?"

"That's my vulva."

"Do you have a permit for this?" he said rubbing me, "It looks extremely dangerous to me. Look if you don't have a permit I'm going to have to inspect it carefully." said the man.

"When you're done being an asshole I'll show you the permit. Did you really need to handcuff me, Giorgio?"

We reached the floor of his office and the man removed my handcuffs, ushering me into the detective agency's office. "What brings you here, Linnea?" he said, sitting down behind the desk and pouring himself a shot of whiskey. Fuck, it was early afternoon.

"Work, of course. I need to find this girl," I said handing him the details written on a piece of paper "She could be anywhere, even South America."

"You always give me ungrateful tasks, Linnea." he said looking at the piece of paper "Usual price?"

"Usual price. The girl is a priority. Then I need a file on these guys. Life, death, miracles, whatever is rotten in the state of Denmark and anything else you can find."

"I take it this is urgent?" he asked.

"Of course it is. In the envelope you'll find an advance for groceries. Moving on to hotter topics, who's the musician downstairs?"

"The blonde?" he said looking out of the window thoughtlessly. From where he was sitting, he couldn't have seen her." An American who's in a bohemian mood. I've only had a couple of chats with her."

"Next time ask her if she wouldn't do a threesome."

"That's a task I'll perform without charging you a penny," he said sipping again from his glass. I went over to his side and stepped over him, sat down on top of the desk resting one leg on one of the armrests of the chair. From where he stood he could see between my thighs and down to my panties. Under the suit I had a pair of black hold-ups that were just waiting to be pulled off.

"Someone promised me a proper search, if I remember correctly," I added just in case he had forgotten to do his duty. Giorgio grabbed me by the calves and walked over to me, placing one of my legs over one shoulder. His hands slipped on my thigh-highs and I felt him grasp my flesh as Giorgio's face rushed in the direction of my sex. He gave me a kiss on my vulva from above my panties "I'm counting on it, I mean on that threesome with the musician downstairs."

"You be a good boy and make me come, then we'll talk."

He moved the flap of my panties with one finger and began to lick my clit; I was already wet from the lift search and couldn't wait for him to take me. I was going to have to go back to the office after all. His tongue sought me out and delved into my openings, tasting the juices that dripped between my legs without restraint. He slipped a finger inside me and had no trouble at all finding what he was looking for and for a few moments he began to rub me. I felt his middle finger inside me and with his thumb he was stimulating my clitoris with gentle pressure and a twisting motion, if he hadn't hurriedly taken me I would have come in his hands. Then he swiftly unzipped his trousers, put my legs around him and I felt the tip of his cock against me. He took me. With Giorgio we had always done things in a hurry, in the car, in a doorway, on that desk, but it suited us both that way. With him I knew I wouldn't have to waste time on preambles, he would fuck me, we would enjoy ourselves and then we would go our separate ways. I could feel him sliding into me, his penis was pounding me relentlessly. I grabbed his bottom and pushed him against me forcing him to fill me with his hard cock until I exploded. He pumped me as we held each other in that precarious position and by now I was on the verge of coming. I felt my sex throbbing, Giorgio knew exactly how to take me and make me come.

I held him tightly as he gasped on my neck, kissed me, and his face was lost in my hair and then I exploded in a cry of pleasure, continuing to claw at his bottom and push him against me. I felt him come and his hot fluid filled me. We remained motionless for a few moments then Giorgio gave me another couple of strokes, while his member quivered inside me releasing those juices that I had tasted before. We stopped for a moment longer, embracing each other, before he slumped down in the armchair behind him. He handed me some paper towels to dry me off and did the same with his gnarled cock. It was bigger than I remembered, or maybe it was my imagination playing tricks on me. I cleaned myself up and hurried towards the exit. By now we had said the important things, talking after that fuck would ruin my mood.

CHAPTER 4

That evening I had a quick dinner and got back to work after Patricia cooked a pasta.

Patricia was a girl I had met on a chat room some time ago when I decided I wanted to know more about the lesbian world. We hit it off right away and for a few months we chatted until she decided to come visit me. She was from Nebraska and was an actress, although acting didn't seem to be one of her priorities. She worked for six months in America and when she had enough money she would come and visit Europe, maybe get odd jobs to supplement her income. She had beautiful long black hair, an 'American' smile as I called it, and was quite attractive. I hosted her for a few months in my flat, more out of curiosity than anything else. By now she was coming and going between Dublin and Milan. Some acting there, some rest here; an arrangement I had got used to.

I began to investigate the bank managers that Liberati had provided me with. I had started on LinkedIn and these guys had no qualms about giving details of their activities on their pages. CVs, the department they worked for, what they did; some even boasted of certain operations which sounded quite illicit. They didn't realise that such information, good for a CV, would reveal so much more to those who investigated them. What amazed me, however, was that they didn't seem to be high enough in the hierarchy to do much damage. I friended them on Facebook and a couple of them accepted, giving me access to more information (my profile picture was a magnet for men, few could resist). It took me a while, but in the end I had an organisational chart of the company, I understood that three characters, two men and a woman, were the ones pulling the strings, and by now I knew life and death of several of them.

I was tired but I couldn't sleep even though it was late at night. I walked around the living room for a while, had a glass of Chardonnay, but in the end my eyes kept going to Patricia's bedroom door. *What the hell*, I thought to myself, *why not?*

I did not knock. I opened the door ajar and saw her in bed asleep. One shoulder was sticking out from under the sheets and was slightly illuminated by the light filtering through the shutters that were not completely closed. I could hear her heavy breathing, I followed for a moment the movement of her chest rising and falling slowly. I undressed, placed my bra and panties on the floor and slipped under the sheets, as gently as I could. She was sleeping in the nude, she was turned on her side and had her back to me. I rubbed myself against her to find a suitable sleeping position, my breasts touched her back and my pubes came into contact with her smooth and generous bottom. I wrapped my arm around her waist and tried to stay as still as possible so as not to wake her up. I could smell the shower gel in her hair and felt her breathing, in contact with my body.

After a few minutes, when I was just about to fall asleep, Patricia took my hand and held it against her breasts. "It took you a long time to make up your mind," she said.

"I know."

She turned to me and we kissed.

CHAPTER 5

After a few days Giorgio Pedrazzoli turned up with a packet which he placed on my desk.

"Here's the information on the guys you asked for."

I took a quick look at the file. "What's your idea?"

"The names you gave me are all half-pints, small players. The ones you're interested in are the last four, those guys are well-connected and, as they say, have power."

Three of the people were the same ones I had tracked down on my own, but the fourth was totally unknown to me, although the face was somewhat familiar. I couldn't place him anywhere, no matter how hard I tried. He didn't even work for the bank, from what I could see from the files. "What about the girl?"

"That will take me a few more days. I'm following a lead but I suspect she's gone abroad."

He scratched his head as if a thought had suddenly occurred and just as quickly slipped away.

"As for the musician, it is a no go, just two-way stuff."

"Did you fuck her?" I asked.

"Obviously."

"Then that means you didn't put enough effort into convincing her. Let me know how the investigation goes." Giorgio left in a hurry, leaving me to my own thoughts. Where had I seen that man in the photo before? Then it dawned on me: I logged on to Facebook and there he was, in a photo with a couple of his accomplices. He turned out to be an Armando Testa, as confirmed by Giorgio's file. I went to his profile, started searching the net and finally, bingo, I had found a link.

"Can you make an appointment with Countess Casati?" I said to my secretary.

"When do you want it?"

"As soon as possible. It's urgent."

After a few minutes the answer came. "You can go today, the countess says you are always welcome, even without having to announce yourself."

Countess Casati was a very sexy forty-year-old woman whom I had helped on a couple of occasions, the first during an obnoxious divorce and the second for the inheritance left to her by her father. Her knowledge of well-to-do circles, not only in Milan but throughout Italy, was renowned, something she cultivated hand in hand with her new passion for beautiful girls. I took the car and drove to her house in the Brianza hills. It was a sumptuous villa, with an enormous park and surrounded by walls. I announced myself at the entrance gate, which opened immediately, and drove up the driveway to the villa. All around me, centuries-old trees, a well-kept lawn as if it were a golf course or a carpet and, next to the house, a young man in his mid-twenties without a shirt, with a statuesque body that would make anyone froth at the mouth, who was taking care of the roses. What a gardener.

I went in and the maid showed me upstairs where Countess Casati was waiting for me in the bedroom. To call it a room was an insult, as it could have been as large as eighty square metres, with a large four-poster bed, a reading area and sofas. The ceiling was frescoed and one could see important paintings on the walls, some modern and some more classical. Countess Casati came towards me and gave me a kiss on the cheek. "Linnea, what a surprise, please have a seat," she said motioning to the sofas by the window, "How can I help you?"

She wore a black silk kimono with a dragon drawn on the back. She was exactly as I remembered her, with ample curves and ample breasts, though not overweight. She cared about her figure and certainly spent more time in the gym than I did in the office. Her blonde hair was up at the nape of her neck, as if she hadn't had time to tidy herself up.

"Thank you countess, there is one matter..."

"Can I get you a coffee or something?" she said, her eyes searching for a waitress.

"No thank you. I'd like to know more about Armando Testa. I'm working for a client and this guy seems to be popping up all over the place. Obviously on the bad side."

"You won't be able to talk to Armando, even with an introduction from me. Not directly."

So she told me how one day this gentleman had suddenly come out of nowhere, how he had made his way into important circles and had forged links with the most important merchant banks in Italy. He was a fixer, but at the same time he was part of a more powerful organisation, which exploited the importance of its members to carry out shady and almost certainly illegal dealings. Politicians, financiers, a lot of people were in on it and Armando held the strings of this organisation.

"It almost sounds like Freemasonry," I said thoughtlessly.

"But darling, that is Freemasonry. What do you

think the parties you occasionally sneak into are, a bunch of bored swingers? Of course there's a sexual angle to it but the real purpose is to bond the members. The exchange of favours is at the heart of that organisation and the exchange of sexual favours is nothing more than a way to further cement the bond each member has with the sect. You may have noticed how some participate in sexual activities and others sit on the sidelines and discuss."

"I had noticed that but I had always assumed they were people who like to watch."

"That and more. Sometimes you discuss business, sometimes you watch, sometimes you participate, sometimes you exchange favours."

"How am I supposed to recognise him at one of those parties? They're all masked."

"There's a price to pay, my dear. If you really want an introduction." And with that the countess opened her kimono, giving me a full view of her full thighs. She was without panties and had spread her legs obscenely in front of me, as an invitation to make love to her.

"Who's the hunk pruning the roses in the garden?" I asked her in an attempt to gain some time but inevitably my eyes were drawn to the blonde hair on the countess's sex and those firm, pale thighs inviting me.

"Oh the gardener? A Polish boy. I think he used to be a bricklayer. I had this idea of putting sculptures in the garden then I thought, why not have a living statue that moves, does things. A dynamic sculpture to cheer the eye, different every day."

I knelt in front of her, placed my hands on her knees and pushed myself between her legs, kissing her clitoris. "Couldn't you have him around, while I deal with the 'price to pay'?"

"Doing it with the servants? Are you out of your mind?" she said, pretending to be outraged.

"He's not My servant, we can explain a few rules to him."

"Oh Linnea, what can I say? If you really want to." She reached out her hand and picked up the phone to issue orders, I heard her say "No excuses, immediately!" and after a few moments the young man was at the door. The countess signalled for him to come closer and then said, "But he's all sweaty, he must stink."

The man was visibly shocked to see me between the legs of his employer, who was lying halfway on the sofa with her kimono open, showing off all her charms. "Come closer, Konrad," she said waving me over. "Oh my God, Linnea, but he's all sweaty, look at him, he's almost glowing. Konrad," the Countess said, "do you like working here?"

"Of course Countess, I'm very grateful."

"Sometimes, though, one must remember decorum, my dear. What do you say, Linnea?"

"I say it would take a good shower to wash off all that sweat, he's absolutely unpresentable."

The man made to say something but Countess Casati silenced him immediately, pointing to the bathroom door. Konrad didn't understand what was going on at first, so I took him by the hand and we headed for the bathroom. The shower was huge, tiled in white marble and you could walk into it. It would have easily accommodated three people and had numerous horizontal and vertical jets. Once in the bathroom I started to unbutton Konrad's trousers who, at that point, had no further objections. I slipped off his boxers and saw that his penis was becoming visibly hard.

"How uncouth," said Countess Casati, "he doesn't even have the decency to wait until we have undressed."

I took off my clothes in a hurry while the countess sat on a small armchair just in front of the shower. Who knows if she had enjoyed such spectacles in the past. I tested the water and when it was at the right temperature I pushed Konrad in, who in the meantime kept looking between me and the countess. I made him turn around with his back to me and when the jets of water hit us I grabbed some shower foam and started soaping his shoulders. The countess had made herself comfortable, with one leg straddling the armrest of the armchair she was showing us her sex which she had slowly started to caress. I was taking care of that statuesque body and soon started soaping his member, which I felt harden in my hands. It was a nice, big sex that went well with that muscular, defined body. I turned him around and knelt in front of him. That rod was right in front of my face and I kissed him on the head, making him quiver with desire. He looked at me with predatory eyes but the presence of the countess inhibited him. He let me do my thing as I took him in my mouth, sucked him like a madwoman clawing at his massive, compact buttocks, pushing him against me. Every now and then I glanced at the countess who was approvingly enjoying the show, she had stuck a finger in and was fondling her breasts with the other hand. I could see her nipples stiffening under the expert flattery. Konrad was ready, I could hear him panting and so I stood up and turned my back to him, resting my hands on the shower wall and arching my ass in his direction. I could feel his solid member between my legs as he reached for my breasts with his hands, searched my shoulders and hips, lingering on my firm bottom. I was as wet as ever and Konrad had no trouble penetrating me, I could feel him filling me with that hard flesh of his, that massive penis rubbing into me. He held me by the hips and moved rhythmically, pumping me hard, making me wince with every stroke that I waited impatiently for. He penetrated me, rubbing my hard nipples and it was at that point that the countess decided to join us. She stepped into the shower, soaped herself up and then came in front of me. We were facing each other, her back against the shower wall and me facing her. I kissed her while Konrad continued to fuck me from behind, I hugged her, I kissed her neck. Konrad's strokes became more powerful, so much so that I vibrated and clung to my partner. I wrapped my arms around her hips while our breasts danced, in contact with each other, as if a sensual tango was moving them to the rhythm the man was giving us. I felt her generous hips and wanted to kiss her but I was almost on the verge of coming. Konrad heard my moans getting louder and was invigorated even more, moving in and out of me relentlessly. I cried out my pleasure loudly as I rubbed and clung to my partner and then it was his turn. He came and I felt the warm fluids flooding me as his breathing became heavier. He continued to rub against me for a few more moments, and then he stopped. The countess said, "Thank you Konrad, you can go now."

The man said nothing. He got out of me and the shower, took a towel and then dressed with the few clothes that were lying on the floor before leaving us alone.

I kissed her greedily, caressed her ample breasts, sucked her nipples and with one hand searched for her sex which I found completely wet. It was at that point that Countess Casati closed the shower and let me out. She dried me slowly, taking special care of my breasts and then did the same with herself. She sat down on the armchair and motioned me to kneel down. I kissed her hot, wet sex again, sucked her clitoris and bit her protruding lips. The countess held my head in her hands and put her legs on my shoulders. She pushed me against her sex, which my insistent tongue penetrated, making her moan with pleasure. I licked her and fucked her with two fingers, feeling her humours on my tongue. She kept pressing my head against her swollen vulva and I finally felt her enjoyment. The idea of her enjoying me in her hand made me even more excited and I started to touch myself. When she saw me she made me get up and we went into the bedroom where she made me lie down. She came on top of me and again put her sex in contact with my mouth while in turn she started licking my vulva. We continued kissing like that, exploring each other's orifices until we came to orgasm again, almost together. Then she lay down beside me and embraced me. Much later, only much later, when we had finished caressing each other, exhausted, she said to me "I'll call you when I know something, about that Armando Testa business."

"If I have to pay any more prices, let me know, lest I fall into debt," I said laughing.

"Don't worry, my dear, I can always find an excuse to get you into my bed."

I got dressed. It was time to go.

CHAPTER 6

The countess came to the office a few days later. She told me there was going to be another party and had proposed me as a sex priestess.

"As what?" I asked stunned.

"Priestess. Nothing to worry about." Parties were often places to discuss business and she had learned that Armando Testa, plus others from the bank would be present. When they talked about important matters it was necessary to have a priestess, a person who would have sex with them before they started discussing business. It was a tradition, to get caught up in erotic practices before any important decision, the people present would unload their urges on the priestess and get rid of any frustration, making business discussions less tense and as free of conflict as possible.

"And what am I supposed to do?" I asked intrigued by the offer, "I'll be found out immediately if I don't behave properly."

"The priestess does nothing in particular. You put on a mask as usual, please them and then sit with them while they discuss. If you see someone getting more agitated than necessary, if the environment is tense or there are disagreements, you intervene."

"Intervene?"

"Yes, you unzip trousers, lift skirts and hustle until calm returns. In the meantime, you listen to everything they say."

"Sounds interesting. They might talk about something else though," I added thoughtfully.

"There are always risks."

"But do they trust themselves to talk in front of a stranger?" it seemed completely absurd to me that these people would discuss important things in front of anyone.

" I shall say that you are a foreigner and speak little Italian. I'll be your guarantor, so nobody will ask questions."

She gave me the details and the party would be the next day. The address was, again, the house in Corso Como in Milan, where I had attended parties before.

"Can I bring a friend?"

"The usual one who sneaks in with you at parties, the pretty one?"

"That's the one."

"There will be a price to pay," she said, laughing. At my attempt to protest, she added that it wasn't me who would have to pay it, but my friend. I thought about it for a moment and it occurred to me that Federica had never been unbalanced in her bisexuality, even during those wild parties she had always secluded herself with men, no matter if one or more. It would have been interesting to put her on the spot, especially with the countess's cravings.

"No problem." If she had known she would have given me a hard time but I counted on Ms Casati's discretion in such situations.

I made a couple of phone calls to the police station and a couple of acquaintances told me that they were still groping in the dark and that the investigation was going slowly. In this case, no news was good news. In the meantime, Giovanni had been busy digging further into the intrigues of the Banca Popolare Fiorentina and had prepared a big folder for me to study that very night.

The day passed without events and I couldn't wait to get home to Patricia. After that night spent hugging her, not much had happened. We had avoided the subject and any excuse to talk about anything else. But maybe I should have been the one to make the first move. I liked Patricia, but she was something different from all my previous encounters, often dominated by lust, by my search for the perfect orgasm, for the next body to enjoy. Patricia made me feel comfortable, she was a friend but at the same time she managed to intrigue me, to make me want her. A desire that was just waiting to be seized, there at my fingertips, ready to use and yet distant. I couldn't make up my mind, maybe in my heart I knew that if I made love to Patricia I wouldn't get out of it so easily, I wouldn't have the strength to let her go and slip into another bed. Patricia was luring me into a relationship, without knowing it or wanting to, she was slipping me into a dead end from which, I knew, I would never get out.

But would it be so bad to end up in a relationship?

I was contemplating the matter when Giorgio Pedrazzoli came on the phone.

"I found her."

"Are you talking about this Luciana?" I asked just to avoid misunderstanding.

"Yes, she spent a few days in Liguria with her parents and then left for Dublin. I don't have many details about where she lives, but I saw from her Instagram profile that she frequents some homosexual hangouts in the area. How do you want to proceed? I don't think they can easily mistake me for a lesbian." I had to smile. Giorgio was a muscular, big man who often wore a couple of days' worth of unkempt beard.

"Don't worry. Give me the names of the clubs and I'll take care of it."

I scribbled down the addresses on a piece of paper and then started looking for a flight. Then I had an idea.

That evening, when Patricia came home from work at the pub, I walked into her room and said, "Fancy a trip to Dublin?"

She was taken aback. She had been to Ireland in the past and had also acted in some of the capital's theatres and every time she spoke of the place her eyes lit up.

"When are we leaving?" she asked full of excitement.

"The day after tomorrow."

She looked around, she had a lot of clothes scattered around the room, the saxophone resting on the desk. "You don't have to take everything with you, rest assured. I want you back here for a while longer. We're only staying a few days."

She came up to me, hugged me and kissed me on the mouth, "I love Dublin."

"We're not just going there for pleasure, I have some things to do and I need your help."

"And what am I supposed to do?"

I explained to her about the Liberati affair and that we would have to act as investigators, search the various Dublin clubs for this elusive Luciana and convince her to confirm Liberati's alibi in front of the investigators.

"Cool!" she replied, "I can't wait." And then she began to pack her suitcase even though it was a couple of days before departure.

CHAPTER 7

Federica picked me up to take me to the secret party. We had the two masks as usual, but this time Ms Casati had provided me with a new accessory. As a priestess I was to wear a black hooded cloak, which was part of the ritual.

My friend asked me about the novelty and burst out laughing when I explained my new rank of Sex Priestess. "Do you really have to do that?"

"Sounds exciting. Try everything at least once," I replied. I thought about how Countess Casati would corner her in that house. My dear friend was going to try something new herself that evening.

At the entrance to the Corso Como building we found the two usual hounds who checked my pass on my mobile phone and so did two other masked brutes at the entrance to the flat. It was exactly as I remembered it, huge and full of people.

Ms Casati came up to me and kissed me on the cheek, if you can call it that, as we both had masks that half covered our faces. "Welcome priestess," she said, "your meeting is at the end of the corridor, the last door on the right." Then she looked intently at my friend and added, "I don't believe I know you, ma'am!"

Federica mumbled an excuse about the masks and then the countess motioned to the two energetic men near the entrance to approach. They took her by the arms and prevented her from running away while Ms Casati said "Now we shall see, my dear, if you really belong to this group. Follow me."

I would have liked to enjoy the scene but I had a task to perform. In the inside pocket of my cloak I had placed a tiny tape recorder that had been provided to me by Giorgio. In addition, my mask had been adapted and the mole on the left side was actually hiding a micro-camera. I was shitting myself with fear of being discovered.

I arrived in the room and three people were sitting on large armchairs around a small table. I recognised the features of Armando Testa, his lieutenant Mario Gilacci and the woman must have been Roberta Fossati. I started to undress and kept only the mask, putting my clothes by my side and my cloak on the back of the armchair and watched the three of them discussing. Wasn't there supposed to be sex before arguing, I thought? Next to the armchair lay a leather bag. I peeked inside and saw several accessories that would facilitate my task.

The three of them were not paying any attention to me.

"We have to speed up the takeover of the Banca Fiorentina," said Armando Testa, "the more time passes, the more we run the risk of the knots coming to the surface."

"How many million have we embezzled so far?" asked Gilacci.

"At least seventy, all deposited in Swiss accounts," replied Testa. "What's the situation with Liberati?"

"That asshole has gone into hiding! He took a month's holiday and before I could do anything he disappeared from sight. I would have put him down with my own hands, that rat bastard!"

How dare he talk about my client like that? In spite of the mask, you could see Fossati's face was red with anger. She was an attractive woman who I estimated to be about thirty-seven years old. Well-dressed, slim and with small breasts peeking out from under a white blouse. I could see her features and nipples in the half-light. I rummaged through my bag and found the right tool: a fairly large wearable penis, coloured a deep blue. Among the items was some lubricant. I tied the penis around my waist, spread a little gel on the rubber penis, not too much, and approached Fossati. I spread her legs and forcefully pulled off her panties.

"Is this really necessary?" complained Fossati to the other two. Gilacci shrugged while Armando Testa commented, "If the Priestess wants to intervene, she can."

Good, just what was needed. I got her up, mounted on the chair and lifted her skirt from behind. I still had some lubricant on my fingers and I rubbed it on Fossati's vulva. She was dry, probably not expecting such an active Priestess. I felt her clitoris, rubbing it between my thumb and forefinger, making her gasp for a moment, then pushed a finger into her vagina. The finger flowed well, because of the lubricant, which spread well over the inner walls. "Wait a minute..." she made to moan, but I didn't give her time. I bent her over, directed my penis against her sex and in an instant I was inside her. "Ow! Take it easy..." she cried.

Like hell I was going to get sweet on this bitch. I gave her a couple of thrusts with my hips that made her wince, causing more moans, "I don't think so...Ah! Fuck, take it easy."

I had stuck that huge penis inside her and was now clawing at her hips, giving her incredible blows. Every time she tried to protest, I responded with another blow that landed between her legs, making her wince. Slowly she stopped complaining and her protests became moans. With one hand I held her by the hips, helping myself to penetrate her even more brutally, while with the other I sought her sex. She was under me, quivering and moaning, I was pinching her clitoris making her suffer even more, but the bitch was taking a liking to it and was now responding to my caresses. Every time I filled her with that rubber penis, she jerked, moaned and let out little cries that went along with my movements. I rubbed her sex with my fingers, caressed her anus, squeezed her small and firm breasts until I felt her come under me. "Ahaaaaaaa! Bitch, fuck me!" she screamed, "More! Don't stop, make me your bitch." And then I felt her pawing at my attention. I shoved that gnarled cock into her as far as I could and then again pushed with my hips to fill her completely. "Ahaaaaaa! I'm coming!" she finally cried out and slumped down on the couch exhausted.

If it had been up to me I would have continued and taken her anus in the same way, making her scream, this time from pain, but I stopped in time. I was there to watch and listen so I went back to my armchair, waiting.

"Jesus Christ, who sent this one to us?" asked Fossati, not addressing anyone in particular but visibly satisfied with my performance. Then she straightened up and resumed talking to the two of them. 'Hm... I was saying... yes, about Liberati. If he starts talking about our business we're in trouble, we have an unprecedented scandal on our hands."

"Not to mention the risk of going to jail. Did you get the photos?" asked Gilacci.

"You mean the ones taken by our investigator? They're months old, but yes we sent them to him," continued Armando Testa. "Since Liberati has disappeared, if we send them to the prosecutor's office for sure suspicion will fall on him."

"And who will keep him in check then? Once he's in the hands of the police he can always spill the beans about our dealings to get his sentence reduced. Better to keep the photos and leave him in a limbo of uncertainty."

"Maybe it's for the best," said Gilacci, "Who took care of the girl?"

"The investigator." replied Testa. "The only thing that worries me is that Liberati visited a lawyer before he disappeared. We don't know much about that but we're checking it out."

"These fucking lawyers, they should all be put up against the wall and shot dead." Gilacci ruled.

Then I had an idea. I got up and approached

Gilacci. He was in his forties and in decent shape, nothing exciting but not bad either. I unbuttoned his trousers and lowered them to the floor. Then I pulled out his penis and started stroking it. With several naked women roaming the corridors and rooms it didn't take long to get him hard. Then I took Fossati by the jacket and dragged her in front of Gilacci, making her kneel between his legs, pushing her down. I grabbed the back of her head and pushed her against her co-conspirator's penis, receiving complaints in return "You've got to be kidding me, right?" she said outraged.

I didn't care, so I pushed her harder towards her partner's penis until her lips brushed against it. I pressed further and finally she had to take it in her mouth. "Oh Jesus Christ!" cried Gilacci, trying to withdraw from that situation certainly unexpected by the fact that his colleague was giving him oral sex. I continued to guide Fossati in that fellatio until I was completely convinced that she would continue until her partner came.

"I can't believe it, this is a fucking joke!" said Armando Testa.

I went back to rummaging in the bag and saw more tools that I would need. Unnoticed, I approached Fossati again and before she could complain I put a pair of handcuffs on her.

I took a vibrating egg from the bag, one of those

with a remote control, lubricated it slightly and introduced it into Fossati's vagina, who seemed visibly irritated by my attention. I set the vibrator to position three, feeling a familiar buzzing between my victim's thighs, then turned my attention to Armando Testa. I was going to do him, of that I was sure. I unzipped his trousers and felt that he was already hard, probably aroused by the two in front of him. I made him stand up by pulling his penis and sat down in the armchair in his place. There wasn't much to explain, the man was on top of me in one leap and began to penetrate me. I held his legs behind my back and pushed him into me, harder each time. I didn't kiss him but the knowledge that what would have been a bitter enemy, if only he had known who I was, was fucking me in that room filled me with excitement, with a sense of power that was intoxicating.

He kept pumping me with that hard cudgel filling me, I felt him enter me, push me all the way in, come out and then start again. I don't know how long we did it but I came suddenly, followed shortly after by him, who collapsed against me. When he had recovered, I returned to my chair, like a good Priestess.

When the other two had finished, Fossati, visibly shaken, said, "Perhaps we should adjourn this session.

The others agreed and let me go.

Freed from my duties, I felt like looking for my friend Federica. I found her in a room, tied hand and foot to a bed with Countess Casati tormenting her with a vibrator. From the moans of pleasure coming out of her I decided not to worry and to wait until she had finished. With Ms Casati there was never any peace of mind, it could have gone on for hours. I sat down on a small armchair, right in the middle of two young men who were masturbating at the scene; I might as well do something while waiting, so I reached out my hands and grabbed the members of the two, one with my left hand and one with my right hand, which I began to massage. Federica hadn't noticed that I was watching her, sitting while I masturbated those two strangers: all the better. The two let me do it, sometimes urging me to go faster or to slow down. I had nothing better to do than obey.

It was sometime later, when the countess was completely satisfied, that she released my friend.

"Ah, you're here?" she asked half pissed, "Shall we go?"

"Gladly."

We remained silent until we reached the car and then she exploded, "Do you know her, that one?"

"I assume you're referring to the woman on top of you? No, I don't think so, why?" I said with a goody-two-shoes attitude.

"She had two big guys grab me and tie me to a bed. She said I was a gate-crasher."

"Which is true. Did she torture you, poor thing?" I asked her.

"What a bitch you are. She's done it to me, licked me, stuck fingers in places I didn't know existed, made me come in every way imaginable, even better than a man," she said looking out the window as I had started the car by now and was driving towards her residence.

"That doesn't sound bad."

Federica remained thoughtful for a moment, then added, "Of course she had a knack for it; she certainly knew just the right spots to turn me on."

"Not bad. Had you ever done it with a woman?"

"With one like that? Never in my life. I had a few little experiences at university just out of curiosity, but man! There was an abyss. I even had to lick her, more than once."

"Did she taste good?" I teased her.

"Bitch!"

CHAPTER 8

I was supposed to be leaving for Ireland that afternoon, but I had another job to do first. I had arranged an appointment with the assistant prosecutor in charge of Maria Sole's murder and after much insistence I persuaded him to see me.

"To what do I owe the honour?" he asked, pointing to a chair in front of his desk.

"A delicate matter."

I told him how Liberati had come to my office, the attempt to blackmail him, or rather to silence him, and his connection with Maria Sole. I didn't leave out any details.

"It seems to me a difficult position to support," he said looking at the photos.

"I realise that, but I would like you to keep these photos confidential. If I'm right, someone might send them to you anonymously in a few days."

"And you say these three guys are the culprits?" he continued half incredulously.

"These are the papers Liberati provided me with. There's definitely a motive to silence him," I insisted.

"I'll look into it; a good financial scandal would be good for my career."

"Plus there are these recordings, which came to me from a contact whose identity I cannot disclose." He looked at the flash drive and seemed to weigh it up. "I warn you that there are spicy scenes, but the three are clearly recognisable despite the masks. The voices are distinct and they say they hired an investigator who was also in charge of the murder."

"Wow!" he said after glancing at the footage.

"I'm not finished. I'm leaving for Ireland, where I'm told there's a witness who can confirm Liberati's alibi," I continued, "I just need a couple of days to find her."

"A couple of days isn't much time," the prosecutor said thoughtfully, "especially considering we don't have any culprits on our hands. At least, until you've served up two prime suspects on my table."

"A couple of days, that's all I'm asking," I pleaded with him.

"Fine. In the meantime, I can always investigate these three guys. Linnea, I know you by reputation and I know you're not pulling a fast one on me, but if by chance..."

"Don't worry, I don't want you on the wrong side of the fence." We shook hands with a promise to meet again in a few days and then I hurried home, where Patricia was waiting for me.

We arrived at Malpensa late and for a moment I thought we were going to miss the plane - Patricia had brought along a big suitcase, the size of a house, despite my advice to travel light. We sat in first class on a direct flight to Dublin and finally, as soon as we were off the ground, I relaxed.

"You treat me well, first class," Patricia said as she looked around.

"Didn't I tell you? I plan to seduce you," I said between serious and facetious.

"You're succeeding perfectly."

I dozed the whole time and when we arrived Patricia elbowed me, all excited, "Wake up sleepyhead, here we go!"

The hotel was the best I could find, a suite at the Merrion, right in the centre of town.

"No expense spared," she told me as she looked around. It was for all intents and purposes a proper flat. There was a dining room, a room with sofas and a fireplace, a gigantic bathroom and the bedroom. Patricia arranged her suitcase in a corner and flung herself onto the huge bed.

"So you really do want to try and seduce me," she said, laughing.

"Something like that. I figured you wouldn't be embarrassed to share a bed."

"Are you kidding? It's huge, I'll need a GPS to

find you."

We took a shower, each on our own, before going to dinner. The clubs would be opening much later, there would be no point in walking around on an empty stomach.

The first club was called The Level, an LGBT disco bar, with a disk jockey that left something to be desired. We looked around but it was still early and the bartender, when I showed him Luciana's photo, didn't seem to recognise her. We sat at a small table sipping beer and watching the local wildlife.

"Ever been to this place?" I asked.

"A few times, but they are mostly butch. What kind of chick are we looking for?"

"I haven't the faintest idea. I'd say confused bisexual with S&M tendencies," I ventured. Pretty much like me, I thought but I didn't say it out loud.

"Would you like to dance?" asked Patricia after her second beer.

"Why not? Occasionally look around in case you see her."

We hit the dancefloor to the beat that the Irish David Guetta was giving us but after a good hour we decided that we shouldn't waste our time there.

The next venue was called The Standard. This

time we hit the jackpot as the barmaid remembered the chick. She used to come to the bar often, "gin and tonic", she told us. Apparently, she remembered people more by what they drank than what they looked like. We ordered a couple more beers and kept looking around, but after a couple of hours we decided it wasn't happening, and what's more, my head was spinning. We got back to the hotel in the middle of the night and I threw myself into bed without a second thought.

The next day was spent sightseeing like two good tourists in love. Hand in hand, including a visit to the Guinness factory and some obligatory shopping on Grafton Street. I even forced Patricia to try on a summer outfit. She made a lot of fuss but in the end she wore it and was much more feminine than usual. I don't know how but from that point on the ice was broken between us and when I suggested shoes and clothes she listened to me.

We went back to the hotel loaded with bags.

That evening we went out again on our way back to "The Standard" and as soon as we entered, bingo! We saw her immediately. She was in the middle of the club dancing with a girl with studs, shaved hair and a face that would look good on a boxer. I approached her.

"Luciana, my name is Linnea, I'm a lawyer from Milan."

I didn't have time to hear the reply when the studded chick started pushing me, "Hey, you bitch," she said in a knife-edge Irish accent, "she's with me, piss off."

"I just need to talk to you for a few minutes, it's important," I insisted, but the punk was having none of it. She grabbed a bottle from a nearby table and made to hit me when Patricia intervened. She'd told me she'd done judo, and I thought it was to impress me, but instead I saw her grab the stranger's arm, pry her back and knock her to the ground with a dull sound. The people around us made room, mostly to avoid getting into a fight. Patricia hadn't let go, twisting an arm behind her back and shouting in her ear "you better get out of my way before I get serious."

"Do what the fuck you want with that bitch," the punk said walking away as she rubbed her still sore arm. I recovered from my fright and went back talking to her. This time Luciana listened to us. We went to a quieter corner and I explained the Liberati thing. At first she was reluctant to get involved, but when I told her that the man was in danger of going to jail for a long time, she decided that she would come back to Milan to testify. I would pay for her travel and accommodation, of course. We exchanged mobile numbers and promised to meet at the airport the next day.

"You saved my life, my heroine," I joked once outside the club.

"You joke about it but you took a big risk in there." I knew it. My legs were still shaking with fear.

That night we made love.

It was different with Patricia. I didn't feel like I had to have sex at all costs. There was attraction but it wasn't pure lust, and for once I realised I was making love instead of giving myself over to pure sex. Patricia had succeeded where so many had failed: slowly, without invading my space and accepting me for who I was, she had managed to make me fall in love. A lot of people would have been in mourning in Milan.

When we returned, the prosecutor took Luciana's statement and seemed satisfied. He told me to wait a couple of days, when they would announce the arrest of Armando Testa and his accomplices, but that I could let Liberati know that his nightmares were finally over.

I was expecting a fair amount of compensation,

for saving his arse which was, to say the least, burning.

There was still the problem of Patricia. Soon her visa would expire and she would have to return to the States. I could have given her a job and even offered her one, but her calling was acting, not working for a solicitor.

Six months, that would be the period to wait before she could get a new visa.

I picked up the phone and called Giovanni. "Gio, I've decided to take a holiday, after all these years I've earned it."

"No problem, I'll take care of the office. How long will you be gone?"

"a couple of months."

"Not long enough for your friend to get another visa, though," he said, "oh well, you can always take a second vacation, I suppose."

"You're smart. You wouldn't know it."

"I learned from the best."

I couldn't wait to tell Patricia. I hadn't made any longer-term plans but I would definitely think of something once the time came.

******

Book 3

CHAPTER 1

Giovanni had the waiting room syndrome that day. We had broached the subject several times and nobody wanted to give in. I mean, with all the energy spent discussing which magazines to keep on view in the office we could have supplied electricity to half the city.

"What do we keep all those magazines for? The clients all have appointments," I asked.

"So what, even when you go to a primary care physician, they have the magazines; the Cardiologist journal, drug publications and so on. Clients flip through and think 'these guys keep up to date'!"

"OK, but then what did you buy the National Geographic for? If anything, we should have the latest issue of 'Legality Today'," I teased him.

"Well... not everyone is interested in the law. Flicking through a magazine is a pastime while waiting for an appointment..." he tried to explain. Actually, he was reading the National Geographic during his lunch break. I still wasn't satisfied, "I think the National gives you memories."

"What do you mean?"

"Yeah, come on. Did you read the National when you were a kid because they put all those pictures of the tribes in Africa, the little indigenous girls with their tits out? Come on, fess up!"

"Why would you even touch such topics? I could be your father!" he said.

"I used to masturbate to the *Freemans* catalogue when I was a kid. You know, the lingerie section: all those packs, abs, bras that *I see you and I don't see you*. I had no scruples, as long as I could see a piece of meat..."

"But do they still make the catalogue?" he asked in amazement.

"No, now you masturbate on La Redoute. Or on the internet. Anyway, I see you know what I'm talking about."

"Bitch!"

"Actually..."

Giovanni left the magazines on the small table by the entrance and went back to his office. I was about to get back to work when my eye went to the stack of magazines. The Kinsey Institute publication I couldn't pass up, if nothing else it would give me more ammunition against

Giovanni. What the hell had he bought it for? It was a publication of studies concerning sexuality; had he developed a small penis complex?

I'll put this in my drawer, then wait to see if he looks for it, I thought.

I went to the desk and saw that there were no messages, it was going to be a long and boring afternoon. I flicked through the magazine and found an article on debunked myths about the penis. A long list of numbers and statistics to say that large is better than long. A nice Cacciatore Salami is better than a Chorizo.

Then another article on the hardness of the penis, following a survey in Asia. I started reading it; an Asian penis had not yet come into my hands. Or anywhere else.

Apparently, according to the study, there were four degrees of hardness. The lowest level was the panna cotta or overcooked noodle or mozzarella model. Then it went upwards, from the aforementioned frankfurter to banana and finally to the much-loved Cacciatore salami, which was hard, gnarled, rough and straight as an iron.

What the hell is Giovanni reading? I asked myself; I should have studied psychiatry, not law.

It was at that moment that the phone rang: the

persuasive voice of my secretary woke me up from a world of phalluses, measures and hardness in which I was lost in fantasy.

"Countess Casati on line two for you. It's urgent."

"Thank you, dear." I pressed the button.

"Good morning, Countess, how can I help you?"

Countess Casati was known for hosting erotic parties for the Milanese aristocracy, with a dash of Freemasonry and other secret associations I'd lost count of.

"Linnea, darling. An urgent matter would require your attention," she said.

"Certainly Countess, what is it?"

"Oh, not on the phone please. Could you come to my place here in Brianza?"

"Sure, would early afternoon be all right?" I asked.

"Perfect. I'll be waiting."

That's how the countess operated, the word 'appointment' didn't exist in her vocabulary, but adding up all the jobs she had given me I was still in debt. And then the day's calendar was empty; a trip out of town would have done me good.

With the Countess, there was always a price to pay, often of a sexual nature, but I was fine with that: she was a beautiful woman, she knew how to behave and I even liked her. The last time I had met her, I had made love to her and to her Polish gardener whom the Kinsey people would undoubtedly have classified as a "banana".

I arrived at the villa; the gate was opened for me and I drove to the house. A nineteenth-century villa that I used to dream about at night. Old money, inherited from parents and grandparents. Sometimes finding the right parents is everything in life.

Waiting in front of the main entrance was a breathtaking blonde, wearing a little evening dress despite the fact that it was just after lunchtime, and two legs that would have looked good in Vogue. The countess knew how to choose them well.

"Ms Martini. Welcome, the countess is waiting for you," and she motioned me to follow her. She had an eastern accent, almost certainly Russian. I watched her from behind as she walked up the stairs, her bottom swaying before my eyes, and I knew immediately that I had been mistaken. No Vogue, this was a Sport Illustrated main cover. Toned legs, wide but not exaggerated hips, and the moves of someone who has long known she won't go unnoticed.

"Linnea, dearest," the countess said as she saw me enter the huge lounge. She was sitting on a chaise-longue reading a newspaper, and got up to meet me and give me the three ritual kisses. She fooled me every time because I always stopped at the second one. "Please come to the sofa. Dionisiya would you mind having some tea and biscuits made?"

The beauty nodded in assent and disappeared.

"Dionisiya?!"

"Pretty, isn't she? She's from Lithuania, sorry but she doesn't speak Italian very well. By now, apparently, we have to consider ourselves citizens of Europe, so I thought I'd make my contribution. You know, Lithuania has recently been included in the European Community. What do you want, one has to integrate nowadays, one can no longer think of Italy as a country isolated from the rest of the world. Tongues aside, or maybe I should include that as well," she said, laughing, "she's a really good girl."

"I suppose," I said, "Nothing to do with those three metres of thighs she carries around?"

"Well, my girl, one has to fight loneliness as well," said the countess winking at me.

"You told me I'd have to deal with a delicate matter."

"Oh, of course, of course. But let's have tea first, there will be time to discuss business later. Oh, thank you Dionisiya, please put the tray on the coffee table."

The big blonde stood by and the countess clapped her hand a couple of times on the sofa, inviting her to sit next to her.

"You know, Linnea is an old acquaintance, she has helped me several times in dark periods of my existence. Linnea," she said turning to her companion, "this is Dionisiya. Do you know that she is also an Aikido champion in her country?"

"Judo," said the blonde.

"That's it, yes, Judo, you know, one of those Japanese martial arts. I can't tell you, when she gets into it, she wraps herself around you like a python and... but we're digressing here..." she said, laying a hand on her companion's exposed knees, "I called you about the matter of the Marchioness Bigazzi-Tarterini."

It was going to be an interesting afternoon.

CHAPTER 2

"Giorgio, where are you?"

"In a white van marked 'Bettinelli Plumbing Services', just outside Vercelli, why?"

"Shit, with all the work I hand you and clients to investigate, you're reduced to a second job? Where do you spend your money, on hookers and poker?" I asked.

"Ha, ha, ha, very funny. Look, I'm doing surveillance, if you don't mind if it is not urgent..." Giorgio Pedrazzoli, owner of the Pedrazzoli Detective Agency, was visibly irritated.

"Of course it's urgent, otherwise what am I calling the most famous detective company in Milan for?"

"In Italy, you mean! I'm not one of those poor chaps who take photos on behalf of cuckolds!"

"You'd better be, where can I find you then? It's really important!"

The task that Countess Casati had given me was complex and Giorgio was the person who would have done it for me. Minimum effort, maximum profit.

"Vercelli centre, I'll send you a message with the

address. Knock three times on the van and it will be opened for you."

"No keywords, like 'Open Sesame' or 'Abracadabra'? Or maybe 'Zucchini', that would do the trick," I couldn't get that Kinsey report I'd read in the morning out of my head, and now every man was ranked by penis hardness and shape, in my mind. I wanted at all costs to avoid the office and find myself imagining Giovanni's nether regions.

"Look, hurry up, I'm really busy!" the voice croaked through the speakerphone installed on my car, but I managed to grasp that he had an investigation going on.

I shifted up a gear, slammed my foot on the accelerator and entered the ring road. Not wasting time was essential.

When I arrived in Vercelli, I left the car in a side street and headed towards Piazza del Municipio. It didn't take me long to spot the van, I knocked and Giorgio opened the back door.

"Come on, get in!" he said after looking around to make sure no one was watching us.

The inside of the van was much more high-tech than I would have expected. There was some kind of console with three monitors, a laptop, headphones, something that looked like an equalizer and other electronic devilry.

"And you mean to tell me that with all this equipment you don't go spying on couples?" I asked him.

"That, just for fun," Giorgio replied.

He told me about the operation he was conducting. The first monitor showed the outside of the building under surveillance, the City Hall. The second one was placed on the glasses of his collaborator. That micro-camera was a masterpiece of technology; Giorgio said, it cost a fortune, but the results were astounding: sharp images from a component that was, in fact, invisible.

The third monitor received images from a second camera that was hidden in his assistant's briefcase. That one provided a wider view of the premises. The audio came directly into Giorgio's headphones and was recorded, along with the images, on the laptop he had positioned in front of him.

It took weeks to convince the councillor, but he finally let his guard down and agreed to a meeting.

Pedrazzoli was working as an investigative consultant for a construction company. The company in question, Robecchi Cantieri, had won the contract to build a number of council houses and the work had started well, about a year earlier. Then, with the new councillor taking over, the company had been subjected to all sorts of blackmail and prevarication which was now pushing it to the brink of bankruptcy. At first, the councillor had suspended work due to an unspecified investigation. He later accused Robecchi of using substandard materials, which opened a new dispute with the municipality. The final straw came when the councillor accused Robecchi of dumping construction waste in the nearby canal, which was completely untrue.

In any case, all those stalling tactics had brought Robecchi frighteningly close to the deadline for the first batch of flats, and if they did not complete the work there would be penalties.

The last investment before closing the shop was to hire Pedrazzoli Investigations. Good Giorgio was as expensive as lightning but guaranteed results.

"The councillor is in cahoots with a company competing with Robecchi," he explained.

"Is he taking money under the table?"

"That's what we want to establish today. He's certainly hands and feet in the company, which belongs to his brother-in-law. We already have plenty of evidence on that, today we're trying to put the icing on the cake. Giacomo, the guy who's in there, has a proposal that the councillor can't refuse. If all goes well we'll be back tomorrow with the money and the carabinieri."

"Very interesting."

Actually it wasn't, I was bored out of my mind, but Giorgio's services were unparalleled. Which reminded me that he wasn't just good at watching. I reached out and put my hand on his fly.

"Linnea, I'm not the type to back down on such things," he said without moving his eyes from the monitors, "but this isn't a good time."

Like hell I was going to give in to him, I had him in my hand now, literally, and I wasn't going to let go. Besides, in spite of all his words, I could feel him getting harder by the minute.

"Linnea..."

I unbuttoned his fly and, helping myself with my other hand, pulled out his penis.

Zucchini! No doubt about it.

It was a nice, straight, well-proportioned cock. Not too big, but Giorgio knew how to use that tool like a pro. I'd already tried it and when he fucked me he was one of those guys who was really into it, he liked to hit you hard and make you feel it inside.

Giorgio pretended to be concentrating, but I was watching his face as I stroked his penis, and I could clearly see that some idea was going through his mind. Good, I said to myself.

The floor was rough and cold, but I knelt down anyway and made my way between his legs, assuming the position of a secretary.

His cock was right in front of my face, hard and waiting. I grabbed it again with one hand, a firm grip as he liked it, and brought it close to my lips. He wasn't going to get away with this quickly. The tip was warm and smooth, and I teased it lightly with my tongue. Giorgio let a moan escape.

"Come on, be a good girl, I need to hear what's going on."

"What, you men haven't discovered multitasking yet?"

Giorgio let go of a sigh, placed a hand on the back of my head and urged me to continue working. Some women don't like to perform oral sex, but for me having the right member between my lips (or hands, for that matter) stimulates me. I kiss it, discover its taste, feel it grow and vibrate in my mouth. Knowing that through that simple act of sucking a cock I gain control over a man's desires, knowing that he is completely at my mercy, is unparalleled. Good Giorgio was entrusting the most precious of his jewels to my caresses and kisses. It disappeared between my lips, felt the walls of my mouth absorb it, contract against it and then let it go. I knew he preferred me to work the tip, but there was a time for everything. The glans had to be treated with care, savoured like a cake created by a master pastry chef, not swallowed in a hurry. Instead, it should be relished, a little at a time, an ice cream that should be eaten one lick after another. Each time the tongue passes and touches that sensitive part, the taste and excitement becomes more intense, until you reach that moment when you know you could do anything, you could ask the world and the man would say yes, just to not make you stop.

"Fuck, take it easy, you're making me come...Wait...No...Yes...Yes, Giacomo I've recorded everything."

There was a very long pause then Giorgio resumed, "No, absolutely not! Go home, see you tomorrow."

Another pause.

"I don't give a damn. Take a taxi, but get the fuck out!" and then there was silence.

Giorgio closed the computer and made me get up, then sat me down on the sort of console that housed the computer. He grabbed me by the legs while he was still sitting and pulled himself against me.

"Bitch!" he said, "This is an important

investigation."

"Always thinking about work," I said running a finger over my panties, right in front of his eyes, "You've changed, Giorgio, you used to be more forthcoming."

"Bitch!"

Giorgio sank his face between my legs and kissed my sex from above my panties, looked up for a moment as he realised I was already wet, and then pulled back. He was working my legs, the pig, taking it in his stride. God, that two-day-old stubble was rubbing my thighs, Giorgio was kissing the inside of my legs going down to my groin. He brushed my sex and then moved away, his tongue dancing wetly over me, a ballerina pirouetting expertly on the stage of my body. Come on Giorgio, get on with it, I thought, you haven't become a soft romantic over the years, have you?

I took him by the nape of the neck and forced him to kiss my sex. Giorgio took the hint, and with a decisive gesture he pulled off my panties and licked me. My blond hair was waiting, shiny with humours and saliva; his hard tongue repeatedly beat on my clitoris. By now Giorgio knew me by heart, and my pressing against the nape of his neck was only to feel him better, to have contact with his body while he was making me come. He didn't need directions, he knew very well when to play, tormenting my exposed lips, when to stick his tongue inside me and when to stimulate my clitoris. He did a new trick, sticking his middle finger inside me, while with his thumb he rubbed my clit, as if making the money sign with his fingers. His middle finger slid in easily, stimulating my insides, then out to moisten his thumb, which was now firmly planted on my clit. Fuck! That was a first! The thumb was a good idea, I could feel myself being pressed from the outside in. My sighs and moans confirmed to him that the treatment I was undergoing was to my liking.

Giorgio was ready, he lifted himself up and kissed me. I could feel my humours on his mouth, I bit his lip and made him moan. He took me firmly by the hips and penetrated me.

His penis slid in effortlessly, filling me completely as I wrapped my legs around him, pushing him harder against me. Giorgio was fucking me, and in the meantime, he continued to stimulate my clitoris with his thumb. Double treatment, I couldn't complain. I was in a precarious position and on a couple of occasions I even risked slipping under those violent blows. Giorgio then grabbed me by the buttocks and pushed hard, against and inside me. His fingers were holding me tight, I could feel them sinking into my buttocks, and with each movement, after each stroke those fingers were making their way towards my anus. I could feel them dancing around my sphincter, stimulating me further. Giorgio was panting on my neck, kissing it, sinking his face into my hair, while down there he was performing one of his magic spells. My sex was throbbing with pleasure and I knew I would soon come.

"Come on! Harder!" I urged, holding him by the hips and pressing him against me. Sex done well is always a solitary act, even when there are two of us; the partner becomes an object of our pleasure. It's all bullshit what they say about pleasing the partner on duty: in those moments there was only me, the search for my pleasure and my vagina that was about to burst. I could feel the orgasm building up inside me, and Giorgio had known for a long time that he should not stop or slow down for anything in the world. That crucial moment when you feel your sex throbbing, when you know that with each successive stroke the stimulation will get stronger and stronger, was coming. Again, I told myself. One more time, I repeated to Giorgio, don't stop.

And then I came.

I felt my body contract, the pleasure coming directly from my sex to my brain, driving me crazy with pleasure. My toes twitched as they pushed through my shoes. And then it was Giorgio's turn to flood me with his hot sperm.

We sighed and stood still for a moment, then Giorgio moved briefly, gave me another couple of strokes, more gently, as his orgasm wore off. I could feel him pulsating inside me. I could feel that hard penis throbbing and jerking against my walls and then finally letting go.

He gave me a quick kiss and then, still inside me, he looked around for some tissues.

We hurriedly cleaned and tidied up and then Giorgio slumped down in his chair.

"Christ, Linnea! If I were the marrying type, you'd be the ideal candidate."

"And then find ourselves in ten years' time spending the evening in front of the television? No thanks!" I laughed, but there was truth in what I was saying. I wasn't ready for a relationship yet and most of all I was scared of the possibility of a relationship floundering. I tried with Patricia but the distance between us was a serious obstacle. To be able to keep the libido at bay and be stimulated by the same partner for years and years, always in new ways was a feat I didn't think possible at the time.

"Shall we go for a beer instead?" I proposed, "after all there's some business to discuss as well."

"There's a pub just around the corner."

"That'll be great!"

We got out of the van and walked to the little bar. My legs were shaking and I took Giorgio under my arm. Not that he was any more stable than I was, after that standing fuck, but we made do.

"So what's this all about?" he said after the waiter put two Coronas on the table, complete with lemon in the neck of the bottle. I took a sip and explained the problem to Giorgio.

"Hmm... Watching all those people will be a logistical mess."

"Even for the best detective in Italy?"

"Eh, yes! You make it easy, but to do a job well done would take months."

"We don't have months," I said handing him the folder Countess Casati had entrusted to me.

"Okay, I like challenges," he said peering at the names in the file, "Something will come to me."

My mind went back to the van in which we had made love. Maybe I'd come up with an idea.

CHAPTER 3

The hospital was outside the city, a clinic surrounded by greenery that could have easily passed as a Hollywood home if it hadn't been for the sign at the entrance. I was in the front seat of the countess's Maybach, next to the driver. Ms Casati was sitting in the back with her new flame. She had reclined her seat and was dozing, while the blonde was watching a film on the screen in front of her. Ms Casati knew how to enjoy life. The seat I was on, I would have wanted it in my living room. Soft, supple, with attention to detail. I thought my S Class was luxurious, but this was another world. You couldn't hear a fly in the air.

The driver dropped us off at the entrance, opened the doors and let us out. The countess was leading the way, having visited her friend several times that week. Dionisiya stood beside her and I walked two steps behind them. There was a hierarchy to be respected in certain places.

As the countess passed, nurses and doctors bowed like slaves before a sultan; it was quite an effect.

We arrived at the room of the Marchioness

Bigazzi-Tarterini. I thought of my little flat in the centre and sighed. The big room was a mixture of old and modern. There was monitoring equipment but also a walnut desk by the window and a couple of leather sofas. Through two half-open doors I could see the cream marble of the bathroom and another room where one or more guests could stay.

The marchioness was a tired old woman, she could have been eighty. She was as thin as a skeleton and had very white hair tied back at the nape of her neck. Her hands were closed like resting claws and on her skin one could see the dark spots left by age. Her face was hard but serene, her eyes were closed.

Ms Casati sat down in a chair beside the old woman, took her hand and asked, "How are you Gemma?"

The old woman did not answer. She turned her head to the side, squinted her eyes and nodded to the countess. She was breathing hard and that little tube bringing oxygen to her nostrils did nothing to detract from the old lady's grace and authority. If nothing else it made her look like an old warrior at rest.

"We're on the couch if you need anything," Ms Casati said. She put the button that acted as a bell in her hand, gave her a kiss on the forehead and motioned us to go and sit down.

"It's a shame to see her in that state. You know Linnea, she was a Priestess once. One of the best." Priestesses were a familiar figure to me. At the various masonic parties at Ms Casati there were always one or more sex priestesses who started the parties and could do whatever they wanted to the guests. I didn't fully understand the rules or meanings, but I had experienced the intoxicating experience.

"What happened to her?"

"A car accident. The driver died and whoever sent them off-road disappeared. The investigators think it was a hit-and-run, some joker speeding in the car and pushing them off the road."

"You're not convinced?"

"Not a bit. When they took her to the hospital she whispered it in my ear 'they tried to kill me' before she lost her sanity," said the countess.

"But who..." I didn't have time to finish and the countess silenced me with a wave of her hand.

"One of the nephews, of course. She had recently changed her will. Her only remaining son died a few months ago, taken by cancer. Gemma is an unfortunate woman, she has seen her three children die in the last ten years. No mother should outlive her children."

"And the grandchildren are on that list you gave me."

"Exactly. If anyone has hurt poor Gemma I want to know! No matter what it costs or what needs to be done. Do you understand me Linnea? I want revenge!"

The countess's face was hard. I would have liked to better understand what the relationship between her and the Marchioness was, apart from probably some Masonic intrigue, scandalous parties and so on. But I had the impression that there was something more going on, it seemed almost like a relationship between mother and daughter, even if Ms Casati seemed too young to be.

"Let me do it, I'm already working on it."

"What do you have in mind Linnea?"

"I'm waiting for some information, then I'll decide on what to do. Countess, may I ask you for the keys to your villa in Portofino?" I added.

"Of course my dear, I'll send Dionisiya to your office tomorrow. A weekend of fire and lust?"

"No, nothing like that, I wouldn't dare. I wanted to visit the villa with a friend, who is acting as my investigative consultant on this matter. Then I'll let you know."

The old woman's heavy breathing, now asleep, could be heard in the room, like the hum of a faulty air conditioner. Her eyes shifted to the old lady.

"Oh, and I'd need a couple of papers signed by the marchioness, to get me up and running. Would it be all right tomorrow late afternoon, here at the clinic? I'd like you to be there as well."

"Sure, no problem."

I left the two women with the marchioness and headed for the exit. I wasn't very good at personal affairs and it was clear that the two aristocrats were old friends. It was better not to meddle too much in other people's private affairs. At least, not on this occasion.

CHAPTER 4

I reread the document for a second time and congratulated myself, a true masterpiece. The litmus test would be to get it approved by Giovanni. He was the only one of us qualified to act as a notary.

"Did you happen to see the magazines I bought the other day?" said Giovanni, peeping into my office a few minutes later.

"No, I don't read them. Were you looking for any in particular?" I waited anxiously for him to confess 'I can't find the one from the Kinsey Institute', which was hidden in my drawer.

"No, I just feel like a few are missing," he said uncertainly.

"'If it was *Quattroruote* maybe some customer took it. I'm always snatching *Airone* and *Vogue* from my neighbour's letter box. She's been in litigation for years because she pays for them and never gets the magazines. She even asked me to help her with the legal stuff."

Giovanni rolled his eyes. "No, I think the magazine *Legality Today* is missing; there was an interesting article in there."

Sure, that's the one!

"Listen, since you're here, would you like to check this will? It's an urgent matter for a friend of Ms Casati's."

"Oh my, her again? She has more tragedies than a Greek play."

"She has a new girlfriend by the way. A stratospheric hottie." I knew Giovanni would perk up his ears. Ah, men and their fantasies!

"I'll take a look at it today and let you know. Email it."

It remained for me to decide whether to make the magazine suddenly reappear or perhaps chop off all the articles and leave only the advertising. I would think about it later.

I called Giorgio on the phone. "Hello."

"Hi," he answered.

"If you're not busy this weekend, you're invited to a luxurious villa in Portofino."

"To what do I owe the honour?" he asked.

"Work. That little project I entrusted to you."

"You still haven't told me how much you're paying."

"The old lady gave us a budget of a million euro."

"Pfiu! Are you kidding?" he said after a moment's pause.

"She has an estate of almost seven hundred million, you see! I haven't decided what your slice of the cake will be yet, but you know I can be generous," I teased him.

"I'll pick you up on Saturday morning," he said hurriedly, excitement rising in his throat.

"Deal!"

A few hours later, in the afternoon, the secretary announced a visit. "There's a Dionisiya Adomaitytė who insists on seeing you. She doesn't have an appointment, though!"

"Send her in, I've been expecting her."

"But the diary..." she tried to object. Hot and precise. Often a winning combination in a business environment; all she needed to do was learn to recognise important clients from time wasters and she'd be perfect. Had she succeeded, she probably wouldn't have remained a secretary for long.

"My bad, I didn't warn you."

"I'll let her through," she said, closing the line. Sometimes it took very little to avoid drama, like apologising.

Dionisiya walked in and, boy, in heels she must have been at least six feet of curves and muscles. Ms Casati had found herself a sex highway, no doubt about it.

"Please sit down," I said, holding out my hand and pointing to the small sofa on the left.

"Let's be on a first-name basis, it's easier," she said in a melodious and sensual voice, "I brought you the keys."

"Thanks, have you been to the villa yet?" I asked as I reached her and sat down in the armchair opposite her. I spoke slowly, trying to figure out how she was doing in Italian, which up to that point wasn't bad at all. Except for the strong accent.

"'Not yet. Tina says we're going on holiday later." The secretary arrived at that moment with the teapot and the good cups. Hot, precise and a quick learner. She wouldn't stay long and would soon be off on new adventures, where no one had gone before. Too bad.

I poured tea into the cups and put a drop of milk in mine. Dionisiya nodded in agreement to let me know she wanted the same. It remained to be seen why she had come.

"You speak our language very well," I said just to break the ice.

"I take a lot of lessons, Tina is very keen on it."

I sipped my tea in silence. Old P.I. technique I'd read about in a few mystery books. You keep quiet and do nothing until your interlocutor, embarrassed by the silence, starts talking.

"You've known Tina for a long time, haven't you?" she asked.

"The countess is a long-time client, of course."

"No, I mean, she's not just a client is she?"

Good question. How was I going to explain to her about the orgies, that I'd shoved my tongue and fingers into her current partner's most sacred holes, that I'd banged the gardener while the countess stood by, touching herself?

"The countess is a unique person and as such she also has needs that are outside the norm." There, that seemed the most reasonable thing I could say.

"She treats me like a servant."

"Does she mistreat you? Or disrespects you?" I asked curiously.

"No, not like that. But she says *do this, do that*, like I'm one of the maids, or if I work for her."

"How old are you, Dionisiya?"

"Twenty-four."

"The countess is past forty. You must have noticed that she doesn't talk like anyone else and lives in a world of luxury and important people. That's just the way she is. But I've seen the way she looks at you, the way she holds you by her side when you walk together and, yes, even the way she addresses you. My personal opinion, she's in love."

"She doesn't seem to show it, though," she said, but doubt and regret at what she was thinking was creeping over her face.

"Instead, you can clearly see it. You could easily

be partners for many years to come. The countess can be very generous, but she is also a fragile woman in a way. If I were in your place, I would make some compromises, I would take it lightly, this ordering thing. She's not bossing you around, she's just being herself. Besides, you two make a really cute couple."

"Are you serious, Linnea?" her face lit up as she listened to my words, "It's just that we've only known each other for such a short time. I like her, I risked and left my country to follow her and I'm a bit scared."

"You couldn't have landed better, believe me. If I may say one more thing, be honest with her. She doesn't like to be made fun of, if you know what I mean."

Dionisiya jumped up from the couch and came towards me, hugging me and giving me a kiss on the cheek. "I don't know how to thank you, I don't have anyone here to talk to about such things."

"My door is always open, Dionisiya. If you need me, you know where to find me."

"Thank you Linnea. I have to go now."

She got up from the couch, shook my hand and walked towards the exit. Then as she was opening the door, she paused for a moment. "Oh, there's one more thing. Tina said to tell you that about this job for the marchioness, 'there will be a price to pay'. I don't understand what that means."

"Don't worry about it, and thanks for the message." I understood what those words meant: one of these days my tongue was going to meet the countess's lips. And not the ones on her face.

CHAPTER 5

"Giovanni, are you ready?" I asked leaning into his office.

"Yes, all printed and correct. But are you sure about this matter? There were a couple of weak points I had to strengthen, but the document is solid."

"Great! Come on, let's go they're waiting for us."

At the clinic Ms Casati was waiting for us. The marchioness didn't look strong but at least this time she was lucid.

"Gemma", said the countess, "this is the lawyer Martini and she is accompanied by the notary Caruso."

The old woman nodded. Giovanni asked a few routine questions to make sure the marchioness was lucid. She was. In spite of her age and derelict appearance, the old woman was as alert as a lark.

"This is the new will," said Giovanni handing over the first document, "and this transfers control of all financial arrangements. Marchioness, do you realise that you are passing everything you own under the control of the countess and the lawyer Martini?"

The old woman turned to Ms Casati and said, "Do you realise, they didn't even come to visit me, the ruffians." And then turning to Giovanni, "Of course I understand, that's what I told you to write, isn't it?"

"Um, of course," Giovanni replied in embarrassment. Then he started reading his copy of the documents. As he read, the old woman nodded and smiled. She had a mocking grin on her face, like an old clown preparing a last joke before the last show.

The marchioness had a pen handed to her and signed the documents, then she took me firmly by the arm with those skeletal hands, "you will find them and make them pay, won't you lawyer?" she asked with a mixture of anger and prayer in her voice.

"Of course marchioness, that's why we're here!"

"Good! Good!" and then she let go of me, slumping down on the bed. The poor marchioness was exhausted.

We sat down on the sofa and Giovanni took the floor, "I'll take care of getting the companies and funds transferred."

"How do you want to proceed?" I asked.

"A game of three cards. As long as the marchioness is alive there are no problems," he said quietly, "the trouble might come in case the relatives challenge the will after her death. In that case I have prepared a little joke. The controller of the estate, this company here,' he said, showing us a name on the paper, 'I make it a subsidiary of a company in Panama. In turn controlled by one in the Caymans, going through one on the Isle of Man which is split fifty ways over other companies controlled by... well you get the picture. It's going to take decades of international approvals before they get to the bottom of this, and since we're not talking about criminal activity, no shortcuts."

Giovanni was a genius; if he'd had more ambition, he could have become a billionaire with those tricks of his. Or go to jail for a long time. Either way, I was glad he was working for me.

"Aren't we putting the countess at risk?" I asked.

"No, yours and her name only appear in the last document, which goes into our safe deposit box. If you don't open your mouth, it will be decades before we get it spat out through legal channels. Which are very unlikely."

"Good work!" said the countess. "Linnea, keep me informed of developments, I want detailed reports on everything. I'll read them to Gemma personally as bedtime stories."

"You bet. It will be a pleasure."

On Saturday morning Giorgio came to pick me up from the house; I had already packed my bag for the trip and was looking forward to getting down to business. I went down to the street and found him waiting for me on the doorstep, where he gave me a kiss on the cheek.

"Are you kidding me?!" I said.

"What's wrong?"

"Do you really want to go to Portofino in Mr. Clean's van?" I said pointing my finger at the vehicle double-parked under the house.

"Come on, I need a lot of tools. Fuck, I don't know what I'm going to need yet, I need to see the place first. If I bring all the equipment at least we won't make the trip for nothing."

"Do you even have a radio in that thing?"

"Of course! Even the air conditioner," he laughed.

"If I get a flat arse, after two hours sitting in that ruin, I'll sue you."

"Let's buy a pillow at the gas station. Come on, time is money, get in!"

I got in the seat next to him and I thought better of it. It wasn't bad, it was high enough to give a good view of the traffic. Maybe I should have swapped my Mercedes for a Range Rover.

The villa was FABULOUS! Giorgio went out to open the gate and then drove down to the house. A well-kept garden, the house was a nineteenth-century villa in yellow, on a hill, from which there was a full view of the town main square and the marina. Fuck, I should have been born a Lithuanian with three metres of legs!

"She treats herself well, your countess!" said Giorgio.

"Have you seen the terrace?" I said after unloading my bag and fiddling with the lock. "Even from here the view is wonderful, imagine sitting up there with a bottle of white and soaking up the sun. We're in the wrong business, my dear."

"Tell me about it. Come on let's give these rooms some air. Are we cooking tonight or dining out?"

"If you cook, I'll stay on the terrace, otherwise we go outside. Like hell I'm going to tinker with the cooker. This weekend I'm playing the countess!"

"OK, but at least we have to get a few bottles of wine. I'm not staying dry."

"You think a place like this is going to be short of wine?! Come on, let's go and explore the cellar, but for now let's get on with it!" I said.

"We're fine!" shouted Giorgio from the kitchen. "Two bottles of the good stuff in the cooler and a rack full! Are you sure the countess won't be offended if we vampirize her cellar?"

"Don't worry," I shouted back from the terrace, "We can buy some bottles tomorrow."

God, what a sight it was presenting before my eyes. What the hell was Ms Casati doing in Brianza with a villa like this?

Giorgio arrived with an open bottle and two crystal glasses.

"Thanks. Did you bring the files?" I asked.

"In my bag," he said, placing them on the coffee table; I had already taken off my shoes and sat on the sofa, "I'll be back in a minute."

Giorgio came back with a laptop and a file almost a foot high. How on earth he'd managed to put it together in such a short space of time was a mystery I'd have to read it over the weekend.

"So, who's first on the list?" I asked, savouring my chardonnay.

"The first is this Roberta Ferrari; she lived in Lübeck until a couple of years ago and moved to Milan with her husband. A semi-professional volleyball player, she's a fan of Germany and all things German..."

"Even cappuccino in the evening?" I intervened.

"Those are the Americans! She has a high position at Deutsche Bank; married to Valerio Ferrari, in an open relationship. The good Valerio has a furniture factory."

"What do you mean by an open relationship?"

"That her husband is an errand boy. The good Roberta fucks whoever she wants, left and right and centre, she bosses him around and he says nothing. The poor guy is terrified."

"How on earth did you get all this news in such a short time?" I asked in amazement looking at the photo of Roberta. A beautiful woman in her thirties, short brown hair, great bust and wide hips in a suit that was one size too tight. The photo showed her standing next to a white BMW talking on the phone.

"The more important they feel, the more they expect others to do something for them. Like security. The answering machine has the standard pin, we put a sniffer on the ADSL and a bug on the lapel of her husband's jacket."

"Sounds a bit illegal. What the hell is a sniffer?" I asked.

"A gizmo that you install on your network cable. Sucks up all the data, browser, email, everything. Takes time to sift through but it's a technological marvel."

"Who's second on the list?"

Giorgio handed me more files. The second grandson was an attractive, tanned man in his mid-thirties. The picture showed him in a suit and tie.

"Is that all?"

"You can't always get lucky. We're still working on it. You're going to love this one!"

He handed me some papers and photos. A light brown woman in her early twenties, dressed casually in jeans and a blouse but with a Burberry bag and Jimmy Choo on her feet. Not very tall but definitely attractive and fit.

"What about this one?" I asked Giorgio, but not after sipping some more chardonnay and taking a look at the view. You could hear the trees moving, a gentle breeze was coming from the sea and the sun was high and warming the skin. My definition of paradise.

"That's granddaughter Julia."

"What's so special about her?" she was cute but I couldn't see anything in the files that was relevant.

"Wait!" said Giorgio opening the computer, "this needs to be watched." He fiddled with it for a few seconds and then started a movie. FUCK! I couldn't believe my eyes.

"You have to give me a copy of this one, I'll put it in my report to Ms Casati!" I said snickering.

"Well, then give her these too," good Giorgio was full of surprises: he had pulled out printouts of Facebook conversations between her and a guy called Alexander. Hot stuff!

We went through all the others and it was evening. To go down to Portofino there was an asphalt path which then turned into a steep flight of steps. We found a restaurant with a view of the sea. What more could one ask for?

"What's the plan for tomorrow?" I asked Giorgio as we waited for a house-sized serving of seafood.

"I have to place the equipment. It will take me all day and maybe even Monday to finish."

"If you stay, no rave parties in the villa, alright?"

"No, the rave party was planned for tonight."

"Just keep those cameras of yours in your bag," I joked, but not too much.

"What do you think, I don't have any home movies of you of my own?" Giorgio gave a hearty laugh. I couldn't tell if he was joking, but knowing him there was a chance he might.

"Then tonight I'm going to have to seduce you into spitting them all out. Every last one."

"I'm counting on it!"

I don't know what happens to other people, but for me after a fancy dinner in a great place, the knowledge that I would have to go back to a fabulous mansion with a hunk like Giorgio, made my libido ignite.

I think it was the same for him, in fact while we were going back to the villa, at a snail's pace because after all that food and wine he was getting wobbly, Giorgio was sticking to me like an octopus. I don't know why I never got involved with him, I mean permanently. A steady couple going to the cinema on Saturday nights, cooking together on Friday nights and spending every night in the same bed. Giorgio certainly knew how to satisfy me and he attracted me. I was also sure it was the same for him. Perhaps the problem lay in the fear of routine. I wouldn't have missed my search for the perfect cock, that much-vaunted salami, hard and gnarled, filling you up until you felt full. Maybe what scared us both was the risk of becoming like everyone else, the one that sit in front of the TV every single night. The routine of coming home from work and telling, or worse, being told about past misdeeds, the wrongs you've suffered without actually being able to do anything about them. The queues on the motorway on holiday, with the children screaming in the back seat and having to go on vacation when everyone else does. There was nothing wrong with a 'normal' life. Many people, my parents first, had lived an ordinary one, no frills, but at the same time dignified and happy. I would probably die a spinster and alone like a dog, but at that point in my life I didn't really care.

Giorgio opened the door and I went to lie down on the sofa.

"Would you like another drop of wine, courtesy of Countess Casati's cellar?"

"Why not? As long as you don't take advantage of me while I'm drunk. You wouldn't want to jeopardise my virtues, would you?"

"I wouldn't think of it," he said as he headed for the kitchen. "Tell you what, how about a Refosco from Miani? Fuck these go for five hundred euro a bottle!"

"Sold, I don't know what you're talking about but five hundred euro sounds good!"

He returned with two glasses and the uncorked bottle. "They should let it breathe, but whatever!" he said.

"Whatever!" I replied, pouring half a glass down my throat. Damn, it was the good kind! At that point I only had one thing in mind, wine or no wine, to end the evening.

Giorgio didn't make me beg.

CHAPTER 6

We woke up early and while Giorgio had started setting up the cameras and his gadgets, I was lying on a sun bed on the terrace soaking up the sun. I had been re-reading the files of the marchioness's nephews and nieces, their partners and there wasn't much else for me to do that day. Apart from writing the report for Ms Casati.

The phone rang.

I looked at the display of the phone, it was Federica. "Hello, beautiful, what are you up to today?"

Federica was an old friend. We had met years ago and like me she had a dark side, although hers was still tame. She knew how to let herself go but not completely; I had seen her transformation, little by little, into a semi-savage woman during one of the countess's orgies and, how to say, she was getting rid of the modesty and composure that had characterised her up to that moment.

"Oh, nothing," she replied, "All normal and boring as ever! Shall we meet for pizza this evening?"

"Um, I'm in Liguria."

"Relaxing day?" she asked.

"No, I'm working. Countess Casati has lent me her villa in Portofino and I'm here with Giorgio. I told you about Giorgio, didn't I?"

"Bitch!" she said bluntly, "and you don't even invite me?"

I began to think of an excuse, but deep down I knew she was right. I had got caught up in the excitement of work and had neglected important things like inviting a friend. Giorgio passed by the terrace and headed for the pool. He was shirtless, all sweaty and carrying a duffel bag full of tools. It was a beautiful sight; half-naked men working hard, I could spend my days watching them. An idea was popping into my head, then it took shape.

"Listen, would you like a job as a waitress?" I asked her point blank.

"It's what I've always dreamed of. Years spent on books, a degree, a career, but I know that's my true calling. Linnea have you lost your mind?"

"Not really, listen..." I told her about the plan that was forming in my mind, and the more I talked to her the more ideas swirled around in my head.

"You're kidding, right?" asked Federica when I was done.

"Not even close. Never been more serious in my life."

"Fuck! Count on me then, when do we start? I'll take holiday or go on sick leave, but I don't want to miss this one!"

"OK, see you tomorrow and I'll tell you the details."

"Bye."

I put the phone back down and Giorgio was looking at me shaking his head. "You're dangerous when you get down to it!"

"What do you say, could this work?"

"I think so. What's this friend of yours Federica like?"

"Hot and bloodthirsty."

"I'll send you a resume highlighting my skills as a butler, then," then Giorgio gave a hearty laugh.

"Look," he continued, "we could use a base. Even a little place to rent. No hotels because I need to install a satellite dish to receive the data. Oh, and it has to be in line of sight with the villa."

"Sorry, but with the internet and all that, why..." the sentence died in my mouth as I saw Giorgio's icy stare. I was paying a professional and I shouldn't have questioned his demands. "OK, OK, let me see what's available." Goodbye sunbathing, I went to get my laptop and started searching.

After a couple of hours spent surfing the internet,

making phone calls, apologising 'for calling on a Sunday but it's important', I finally reached the target. A villa just opposite the Casati's was available. Okay, I had promised to pay in cash, I had sworn that it was for an important businessman from the Middle East and that, if things went well, I would rent the villa for several months. At almost ten thousand euro a week, it was an offer that would tempt anyone.

The machine was in motion and would not be stopped easily.

CHAPTER 7

The countess leafed through the report I had compiled.

"There are some very interesting things, but there is still a lot to do," she said with the disappointment that usually appeared on her face when things did not go according to her expectations. Almost ever.

"Besides, why put them all in the villa for a week? What do you hope to achieve?" she continued.

"The idea is to see how they interact, get a profile out of them. There are too many people and we wouldn't be able to monitor them all in a short space of time. The only way is to put them all together," I explained.

"Ending this as soon as possible is crucial, Linnea! I promised Gemma personally!"

I took a breath. The first answer I could think of was 'we've only been working on it for a few days' but that excuse wouldn't work with the countess. The time had come to pull the rabbit out of the hat.

"There would be another reason, to put them all together," I said.

"Let's hear it!"

"I'll show you," I said, pulling the DVD out of my bag, "there's a film of one of the granddaughters that will perhaps serve to bring clarity. Is there somewhere we can watch it undisturbed?"

"Well, there's the little telly room downstairs. Come on, I want to figure out exactly what the plan is."

The countess didn't waste any time, she stood up abruptly, took the DVD from my hands and started walking in the direction of the stairs. Dionisiya and I, taken aback, ran after her.

Calling it a small room was a joke! It was almost as big as my flat, and had two sets of sofas. The first, in the middle, had a cinema screen in front of it, which would have made quite an impression at the Odeon. The second set of sofas was at ninety degrees and faced a huge television; the label said seventy-eight inches. The countess fiddled with the controls, inserted the DVD and the film started seconds later. She went and sat down on a sofa and Dionisiya and I sat on each side.

"That's Giulia, one of the granddaughters," I explained. The countess agreed. The woman on the screen was sitting in a brown leather armchair, explaining to an anonymous audience that she would accept any punishment or command given to her. She was aware of what was going to happen and stated it openly.

The next scene showed Giulia in the centre of a large room. Men and women were sitting on sofas and armchairs arranged around her and watching her.

"Get undressed!" said a male voice off-screen.

Giulia lowered her eyes to the floor and unbuttoned her blouse.

"Slower!" thundered the voice.

The girl obeyed and continued to undress, remaining in her bra and panties. She was tall and thin but with nice proportioned breasts and two beautiful legs. She was wearing beautifully made black lace lingerie.

"Walk!" ordered the same voice. Giulia, still keeping her gaze down began to walk around the room, passing in front of the spectators. The sofas and armchairs were arranged in a circle and Giulia walked in front of them, in a circle, as if she were a slave ready to be sold.

"That's her cousin, Roberta Ferrari!" I said, pointing to a woman in a suit who was framed for a few moments, sitting on a leather armchair. In her hands was a wicker whip.

The countess nodded but did not say a word. When Giulia was back in the middle of the room, a man in a suit and tie stood up and put a collar on her, which he then secured to a black leather and metal leash. Giulia shivered for a moment at the contact with the cold links of the leash beating against her back. The man led her in a circle for a second round. The approval of the audience was evident. Someone was exchanging comments.

"Kneel down!" said the man who was leading her and Guilia obeyed. With a tug on the leash, he made her lose her balance, causing her to fall heavily to the ground. The woman barely had time to pull herself together when the jailer started walking again, dragging her along. Giulia could do nothing but follow him on all fours, like an obedient dog. On the third lap, some of the guests reached out their hands, some brushing her hair as she passed, some stroking her bottom or her back.

The countess was all eyes; up to that moment she had kept her hands in her lap but at that point she extended one on Dionisiya's knees, caressing them with slow circular movements. The Lithuanian did not make a move, as if she were watching a documentary on hamsters for the umpteenth time. Her face was impassive and even a little bored.

Giulia, in the film, had lingered near a woman and was licking her feet while her partner, sitting next to her, got up and pulled off her panties. Not without pausing to caress the poor woman's bottom, he sat back down and watched. A woman got up and unhooked her bra; as she was on all fours, it ended up on the floor covering her hands. Another man reached down and stroked her sex from behind, distracting her from her duties. Giulia was brought to order by her master, with a tug on the leash. The nearest spectators had started to touch each other between the legs.

I glanced to my left and the countess seemed transfixed, not a muscle moved in her face and her eyes were fixed on the television. A different thing was happening with the companion. The countess's hand had slipped between the Lithuanian woman's thighs and was going up and down; with those movements she had moved her skirt; the companion, was lying low on the back of the sofa. This time her eyes were closed.

The scene on the screen continued and slowly some of the guests took off their trousers, some women had their skirts up and their hands inside their panties.

It was at that point that her cousin Roberta entered the scene and gave Giulia's bottom a whipping, making her cry out in pain. She had hit hard and a red mark appeared almost instantly on the poor girl's bottom. She stroked her back, backsides and sex with the whip, giving her a false sense of hope, and then hit her hard on the other buttock. You could clearly see on Roberta Ferrari's face the will to hurt her cousin, the contempt in her gaze was evident and when she hit her, the unpunished pleasure of being able to beat her at will showed like a grin on her face.

Next to me the two women had wasted no time. Ms Casati had grabbed Dionisiya's nearest leg and crossed it over her own. The blonde was completely spread-legged and the countess was caressing her with her full hands, even though she kept her face on the screen. One hand grazed her full thighs while the other was sunk into her panties. Dionisiya kept her eyes closed, biting her lips, caressing her breasts from above her blouse.

I felt myself getting wet. Oh God, I was no stranger to such experiences but I would challenge anyone to remain professional with a little film like that on a giant screen and the two next to each other touching as if they were alone. I felt like stroking myself but realised that this was not one of the countess's parties, where everything was legitimate. Here I was a guest in her house. I tried to contain myself and tightened my legs.

In the meantime, poor Giulia, on the screen, was kissing members, licking feet and being harassed. The owner continued to lead her around on a leash following the guests' requests.

Some were given oral sex, others merely tweaked her nipples or buttocks as they passed, some hit her or insulted her severely. A woman took off her panties and pushed Giulia's head between her thighs forcing her to lick her sex while a man penetrated her from behind.

Countess Casati made her companion stand up, removed her clothes and made her lie down on the sofa. The Lithuanian woman's feet were a centimetre from my hips. She kept her legs bent and lay on her stomach waiting for the countess to finish undressing. I could see her sex, the platinum blonde hair just half a metre from me, her firm, muscular thighs. She was a wonder of nature. The countess was on top of her a few moments later, completely naked. She had sunk her face between her legs and, judging by the moans of pleasure, Dionisiya was licking her sex in turn. The exposed back of the countess was a wonderful sight, the slight contrast between her fair skin and the tanned skin of the blonde beneath her made me wet, it was a heavenly sight, two bodies wrapping and rubbing each other in search of pure pleasure.

Ms Casati, still intent on kissing Dionisiya's thighs, reached out a hand in my direction, slipping it under my skirt. She was silently inviting me to participate in this encounter. It didn't take her long to reach my sex and discover it completely wet. The countess looked up at me for a moment, smiled and invited me to give my contribution.

In a moment I plunged between Dionisiya's legs, my tongue fighting against the countess's to reach the Lithuanian's sex. I hurriedly took off my clothes and joined the two. I kissed a breast, grazed a firm bottom. I didn't know whose fingers were sneaking into my vagina and at that point I didn't care.

CHAPTER 8

The film was long over, I had one of Dionisiya's thighs on my belly and was admiring her wide hips and a bottom that looked like a sculpture. Every now and then I followed its shape with my fingers, now relaxed and satisfied. The countess was on the opposite side of the sofa, exhausted, close to my feet.

I wanted to stay in that position for an eternity, nothing in the world would have convinced me to move Dionisiya from above me, especially now that she seemed to be asleep. What a woman; Ms Casati had chosen well and I had even learned a couple of new tricks. I would have slept there the whole time but the countess, on all fours, reached me and put herself between me and the backrest. She was still sweating and her hair was out of place. She gave me a kiss on the mouth and then said, "I don't understand what the little film we've just seen has to do with the plan you have in mind. Anyway, this DVD stays with me, I want to see Gemma's face when I show it to her."

A mocking chuckle escaped her.

"Giulia and Roberta are already on this film. I

have two trusted people who can circulate freely among the group once in the villa. The other guests are all good-looking and I was wondering if, with the right motivation, we couldn't push them a little further. Maybe we could use one of the priestesses or, if there is one, even a sex priest, if I may dare."

Ms Casati thought about it for a moment, a sardonic smile appeared on her face, and then replied, "I guess that could be done! What do you have in mind?"

"While they are all in the villa, we can hear every word they say, even when they are intimate, and we can observe their every movement. Since they will all be in one place, the team of Giorgio Pedrazzoli, the investigator, will have time to go to each of the guests' homes and sift through papers and computers for evidence."

"And if nothing turns up?"

"Then we'll have to come up with some other plan, but then it will take time."

"Which we don't have. I like it, Linnea! How about my new companion?" she asked, stroking the back of Dionisiya who was still sleeping.

"A born priestess!"

Federica was waiting for me at the entrance of

the pizzeria and after the usual greetings we went in.

"A table for two..." she said.

"For three, please," I corrected her, receiving an astonished look in return. "My friend Giorgio will be joining us shortly."

"You mean, THE Giorgio? The sex machine? The indefatigable vagina investigator who's on you like a fly on honey?"

"The very same!"

"To what do I owe the honour?" she asked in amazement. Since they would be posing as maid and butler in the villa, getting them acquainted ahead of time seemed due.

"He started a career as a butler in a villa in Portofino."

"Will he be there?!" she asked in amazement "Is he off-limits? You're not going to make me jealous?"

"But no, Giorgio is an old friend. Well, not really, but you know..." Federica wasn't listening to me. She was looking at the entrance as if a little girl had seen her favourite pop singer enter the restaurant. I turned around and knew immediately what had attracted her. A hunk with a two-day stubble, black curly hair, in jeans and a leather jacket had entered the restaurant, sending her hormones into orbit.

"...And that's Giorgio," I said gesturing to him for attention.

"Are you kidding?" she said softly, "With a guy like that I would..." she stopped mid-sentence as our host was now near the table. We greeted each other with the customary kisses and I made the introductions. Giorgio ordered a beer.

"Everything OK at the villa?" I asked.

"We have more cameras than Big Brother and that little villa you found now looks like the command bridge of the Enterprise. Monitors, computers, everything you need. I have two operators who analyse everything in real time and make a summary, video and audio of the day: Channel 5 sucks me off! And you can go whenever you want and enjoy the show live," he said proudly. Federica couldn't take her eyes off him, so I kicked her under the table.

"Amazing. By the way, there will be reinforcements. A priest and a priestess, kindly offered by the countess," I said.

"Do they know how to behave?" asked Federica.

"The priest doesn't have a name, everyone calls him *Birillo*. See for yourself."

"*Birillo*, as in a bowling pin? Don't tell me how he got that nickname, I can imagine…"

"How do we get them into the villa?" asked Giorgio.

"You mean the guests? Don't worry, I've already sent out the 'summonses'. All we had to do was to say that it was the marchioness's will, specifying on the letter the seven hundred million estate. Almost all of them have already replied, except one. They'll be at the villa Monday morning."

"Damn easy to convince!" said Federica

"The day after tomorrow I'll have the full report on the others. My people are working day and night to put the information together. I've seen the preliminaries, and there are some very interesting things," said Giorgio.

The pizzas arrived shortly afterwards.

I expected Federica to pretend at some point that she had sprained her ankle to convince Giorgio to take her home, but I realised there was no need. The two of them were hypnotised, they couldn't take their eyes off each other and laughed at each other's jokes. Hands rested on forearms to emphasize a comment. The two of them would have ended up in bed that same night, no doubt. Who knows if it had been a good idea to introduce them, but they seemed perfect. I pretended to get an urgent phone call and excused myself, disappearing into the night.

CHAPTER 9

At exactly eleven o'clock on Monday morning, the first guests arrived. The marchioness's grandchildren were to spend the whole week in a villa that was fully guarded in all respects.

Roberta Ferrari and her husband Valerio got out of a white BMW. They looked around approvingly and told, no ordered, Giorgio and Birillo to take charge of the luggage, while the two of them would inspect whether the villa was to their liking. Giorgio grabbed a valise, looked towards the window from where I was observing the scene and gave me a dirty look.

Federica, wearing a beautiful blue and white maid's dress, perhaps a little short in the skirt, made them sit down in the living room.

Shortly afterwards Giulia and her husband Sergio arrived, followed by another couple. I leafed through Giorgio's dossier and recognised Paolo, the marchioness's nephew, and his current companion, a certain Martina.

Next came a guy on a Harley Davidson who turned out to be her nephew Tiziano and then, in an Audi TT, her niece Rossana, a non-professional photographer working in Milan.

I didn't know what they were saying to each other, but I was going to watch the recordings that evening. It was time to go on stage.

Dressed in the best suit available and with a folder in my hand, I entered the room where the guests were gathered. Roberta was the only one standing and was pontificating, the last sentence I heard her say was, "If we all agree with what I said..."

The voice stopped suddenly and she turned to me.

"And who might you be?" she asked.

"Lawyer Martini. I'm in charge of drawing up the marchioness's will..."

"I demand an immediate explanation! Why are we being summoned here instead of Milan? What's all this about?" continued Roberta.

"Sit down like everyone else and listen to what I have to say. I'm not going to waste anyone's time," I replied.

Roberta's face turned purple; her husband took her hand to invite her to sit down but she violently pulled her arm away, visibly irritated. She made to continue but then looked around. The others were waiting, so she looked around for a place to sit, mumbling 'as long as we don't waste time... it seems irregular...'

I sat down behind a walnut desk that had been

placed in the middle of the room earlier and opened the file. I knew exactly what I was supposed to say but I took my time leafing through the papers.

"Is this going to take much longer?" asked Roberta.

"As long as it takes," I said. Then, as if by magic, I turned the page and pretended to find the document I was interested in.

"As you may know, the Marchioness Bigazzi-Tarterini has been the victim of a car accident and is not in good condition. You are the next of kin and the marchioness has instructed me to draw up a new will. She doesn't remember many of you, except by name, as no one has bothered to visit her in the last fifteen years..."

"How dare she!" said Roberta. In the meantime, the others had also started to murmur. Some shook their heads and others looked around for approval. "The old woman would have been covered with affection if only she hadn't been..."

I stopped Roberta before she completed her sentence; "These things are not my business! My business is to complete the will and follow my client's wishes. So be quiet and listen, otherwise you are free to leave."

Roberta Ferrari looked around for a consensus that, at least on this occasion, did not come.

Reluctantly she nodded to continue.

"The marchioness has requested that you spend the week in this villa. Some of you barely know each other, the idea is that when you meet her, you will at least give the impression that you know each other. If you really want to do that, all the better. Next week, as I said, you will spend it with the marchioness who will then instruct me on her wishes."

The participants looked at each other's faces in approval. All except one.

Tiziano, who had been standing by the window until that moment, spoke: "As far as I'm concerned, the old woman can go to hell! Her and her money. My parents, God rest their souls, have thought of nothing else all their lives. Money has ruined my family and my life. I'm not going to be suckered in, so keep your damn money! I've got better things to do than drool over her millions like these vampires! I'm leaving!"

He put his helmet under his arm and headed for the exit.

"If you walk out that door you'll be excluded from the will!" I said, "That goes for you, Tiziano, and everyone else!"

The man turned to me and replied, "Do what you have to do. Good day to you all!" and so he left.

A few moments later I heard the motorbike start up and drive off at high speed.

I resumed reading my document. "For the whole week, you will be confined to the villa. If you cross the threshold for any reason, you will be excluded from the will."

"And we're supposed to stay locked up in here all the time? It's an outrage!" said Paolo. "It's like being under house arrest!"

"As I said, you're free to leave. For those who want to stay, there's a full fridge, a swimming pool, a tennis court and a nice terrace for sunbathing. Do a bit of what you like."

The group had started talking again but by now I had said what I had to say. It was time to walk and get the fuck out of there. I took my files, said goodbye to everyone and left.

In the cottage where the listening post was, Tobias was busy editing the footage.

"How's it going?" I asked once I'd entered the living room, which had been converted into a TV studio.

"Very interesting. I just finished the part where you read the rules for the week and then left."

"What do you think?" I asked. Giorgio had told me not to let his age fool me. The blond boy with straight hair and piercings was smart.

"More than what they say to each other, it's important to notice what they don't say."

"Meaning?" I pressed him.

"Well, the old woman's in hospital. Apart from the first guy who left, none of the others have asked how she is, whether she's dying or has an ingrown toenail. Nobody cares about the old woman, only about the money."

"Make me a DVD of the best bits, I'll add them to my report to the countess. You did a good job Tobias." The boy nodded and I set to writing my report, disappointed that I hadn't caught anyone in the act of plotting or confessing.

Giorgio always said that waiting was everything in these things; maybe I just wasn't cut out to be an investigator. What if none of these were among those involved? What if it had all been a waste of time?

CHAPTER 10

I didn't go back to Milan and instead I stayed at the villa where we watched the guests. Reviewing a summary of the night, prepared by Tobias, took me almost an hour. The guests were relaxing, but other than that, nothing new.

Tobias handed me a pair of headphones and explained the basics of watching and listening to the guests.

"And how are you supposed to work if I'm standing here watching these guys?"

"Don't worry, counselor. I'm following them from the computer," he said showing a nearby workstation with several monitors, "just do whatever you want."

I started pressing buttons but it was total emptiness, no one was doing much except sunbathing.

From a camera overlooking the garden I could see Rossana with a camera, taking pictures of the local flora. The priestess we had hired was walking towards her with a tray. I turned up the microphone.

"I brought you some iced tea, ma'am."

"Thank you, call me Rossana, please."

"Of course, Rossana, I'm Patrizia. Are you a photographer by profession?" asked the priestess. "I would like to be. I've won competitions, I've even sold some pictures but I've never managed to make it a real job." Rossana spoke and meanwhile her eyes wandered around the garden looking for a subject, anything worth photographing. Every now and then she would bring the camera up to her face and snap away.

"I've worked as a model a few times. Nothing serious, catalogues for clothes mostly. But I'd like to do it full time, instead of earning a living as a waitress."

Rossana assented.

"One thing I miss in my photo book is something erotic. But I'm a bit ashamed to take my clothes off, especially in front of a man. With a woman it would be different, I would know that she is not interested in my body but only in the artistic side. Women are more sensitive, I've seen that. They can dig into your soul and bring it to light. If you know what I mean..."

"You explain it very well," said Rossana, "in fact that's what I do. Not just capture images but give them a different dimension, a meaning."

"Would you like to try taking erotic pictures of me? I'm off this afternoon and maybe we could use one of the upper rooms, or the garden. It depends on your inspiration at the time."

Rossana didn't think about it for a moment. A live and willing subject instead of plants and weeds. Besides, Patrizia was really a beauty, tall, wavy and curly hair, a bodybuilder's physique was evident from under her too-short and tight clothes. Who could resist the temptation?

"Late this afternoon will be fine," said Rossana.

"Perfect," Patrizia replied, "when there's grazing light the photos come out better."

Rossana was intrigued by the comment, the waitress knew a little about photography and perhaps they could have even talked about it a little, their favourite photographers, the old black and white versus colour diatribe.

Patrizia winked at her and before she left whispered in her ear, "I'll find you."

I stayed and watched Rossana, who by then had lost all interest in photographing insects and pollen, slowly make her way back to the villa.

Damn, Giorgio had done a great job with the cameras and microphones! You could zoom in, change the angle of view. It was going to take a while to learn, but it was intoxicating to be able to spy on anyone like that.

I changed the frame to the swimming pool.

Roberta and Giulia were lying on a sunbed, sunbathing. Birillo arrived with a bowl of tea in his hand.

"May I serve the ladies?"

Roberta nodded, not wasting her time talking to the servants. Until she noticed that good Birillo was wearing a short-sleeved white shirt from which muscles and tattoos sprouted. A colourful Greek god.

"How do you kill time in this place, cooped up like canaries?" asked Roberta more to herself than to the two interlocutors.

"The owners of the villa often get massages," said Birillo, "they even had me study with a Japanese master. There is also a sauna, but I don't recommend it at this time, too hot."

Birillo had stood right in front of Roberta, wearing a pair of tight blue trousers from which the family jewels could clearly be seen.

"What do you say, Giulia? A nice relaxing massage?"

"Hmm... I'll pass for today, I'll just sit in the sun," her cousin said.

"There are relaxing massages and, how shall I put it, others that help you regain your energy. More stimulating," said Birillo, "they are ancient techniques that have been somewhat lost over time."

"Massage, then. And you! Lead the way," she ordered Birillo after placing a magazine she was reading on the coffee table. The man nodded and walked towards the house, followed by his guest who was admiring his form from behind. I wasn't going to miss this one.

I fiddled with the controls and managed to follow them into a small massage room. It wasn't very big but Giorgio had set up a couple of cameras. There was a couch, shelves with various bottles and a console. There was also a stool near the window.

Roberta undressed completely and lay down on the couch, waiting.

"What kind of massage do you prefer?" asked Birillo greasing his hands with gel. He rubbed them as if he wanted to warm them up, even though it was a hot day.

"What do you recommend?" asked Roberta.

"Well, there are relaxing massages and then you go up a level to stimulating ones. Some come close to actual corporal punishment."

"Those would be good for Giulia."

Birillo began to massage Roberta's back, which she appreciated with a soft moan.

"Does Giulia like punishment?" asked Birillo.

"She can't think of anything else. Just think, for months she's been in contact with this guy on the internet."

Roberta told how Giulia had met this Alexander

at a tennis tournament. He was participating while she was part of the organisers. They exchanged e-mails and one day they chatted. One of the topics was Fifty Shades and Giulia said she was intrigued. From that moment on Alexander took part in the game. Every single day he gave her little punishments. They spent whole afternoons telling each other their stories, but in the end, Alexander gave her commands, some of them absurd, which she had to follow to the letter. It was not long before the remote punishments became live punishments.

"One day Giulia told me about it," Roberta continued, "that this guy Alexander was tormenting her. Oh, don't get me wrong, she had a lustful look on her face I can't tell you."

Birillo assented and continued to massage the guest's shoulders, then asked, "But isn't she married?"

"That came later. I mean, yes she's married but things were a bit slow and Alexander, with his attention made her feel important, desired, wanted."

"It always starts as a joke, in some things," said Birillo.

"Tell me about it, a sacrosanct truth!" confirmed Roberta.

"There is that feeling that if you don't obey, your

partner might leave, sometimes instead you seek attention, even negative attention. The excitement felt in feeling degraded. Very stimulating," said Birillo who in the meantime had moved to massage her legs, "how did you get involved?"

"How on earth...?" said Roberta, turning around and looking into the man's face. Birillo winked at her and continued massaging calves.

"Oh well... she told me about it one day; she was afraid she was somehow unfaithful."

"Unfaithful via chat?"

"Well no, at that point Alexander was bossing her around and they were even seeing each other, but no sex. It sucked, every day she told me about new punishments, how she felt and so on. At a certain point, we were in my house and I didn't know whether to kick her out or to tell her husband everything and I shouted at her, 'cut it out with this story'. She looks at me and says 'is that what you really want?' Roberta paused to enjoy those strong hands that were manipulating her thighs, then resumed the tale, "I say, she was standing there with her head down and obeying like a dog to whatever I said."

"Did you get a taste for it? I mean commanding her?" asked Birillo.

"I don't know, at first. Maybe I just wanted to

make her stop, she was being too much of a pain in the ass with that Alexander thing. But then I tried giving her other commands and she seemed happy to obey. I was more curious about how much she'd take and when she'd rebel."

"Which didn't happen," said Birillo.

"Exactly. And then there was this whole punishment thing. The little bitch would obey but never completely, there was always one little detail overlooked."

"How did she deal with the punishments?" asked Birillo. The man massaged the inside of Roberta's thighs getting closer and closer to her sex. It was a slow rubbing of flesh, a manipulation that would inexorably get her aroused. Then he stopped; he put more gel on his hands and began massaging her bottom.

"Hm, I like this," Roberta said fully enjoying the sensations those strong hands were giving her. "In the beginning the punishments were verbal! Insults. I tried to humiliate her as much as possible then one day, by accident, I started with corporal punishment."

"Did you use objects?"

"Not at first. A slap, I'd get my feet licked, it was a thrilling feeling of dominance, I couldn't think of anything else. How to humiliate her, what commands to give her the next day. A daily search for the perfect slave."

"I see," said Birillo, "A slave has to be trained and educated. That is the role of the mistress, to make sure that the submissive behaves in the best way and receives the right education."

"Exactly! I couldn't have expressed it better. I later made her break off all relations with this Alexander. It wasn't easy, she was tied to those chats, so I had to work harder. Hey! What are you doing?!" said Roberta with a body shot. From the camera I could see that Birillo was massaging her anus.

"This is an Asian stimulating massage. In our culture the anus is a taboo area, touching it creates resistance. But if you let go and relax, letting me do it, you will see the pleasure hidden in this type of massage. The anus is directly connected to the pleasure centre. Through ancient maps of the human body, known to the Chinese for thousands of years, I am stimulating primitive pathways and channels, hidden lines of energy that will make you feel invigorated."

Roberta huffed but then let it happen. Birillo's thumbs were expertly massaging her sphincter, stretching it in every direction; his fingers were dancing on her firm bottom, grabbing her buttocks, squeezing them, following the natural contours of her muscles. Roberta was lying on her belly, looking sideways and moaning, sometimes lifting her hips slightly to better feel Birillo's manipulations.

"What does the husband think about all this?" asked Birillo.

"The husband is a jerk! He's not as incompetent as mine, but he's got a great little slave girl and he's not taking advantage of her. He prefers to run after others. Any woman, no matter which one, as long as she has a hole. He certainly doesn't understand the finer points of certain games."

Birillo had finished the butt massage and now concentrated on the inner thighs, particularly the groin area. Given the angle of the camera, I could not see completely but I imagined he was very close to Roberta's sex. The woman was now completely in his hands, Birillo was pressing her, twisting muscles, touching her sex. Every single movement was accompanied by a moan. When he was satisfied with his work, Birillo removed his trousers and boxers in a flash. The nickname was not misplaced. He climbed onto the couch and stood over Roberta. I changed the frame to the camera on the side. Birillo had resumed massaging her back but this time there was a variation. His member was positioned directly between Roberta's thighs, rubbing against her sex every time he reached out to massage her shoulders. He scoured her with his hands and a hard, gnarled member; Roberta spread her legs slightly to feel him better.

By then I was soaking wet, I wanted to masturbate but good Tobias was still at work not far away. Perhaps I could have slipped a hand up my skirt, hoping not to be seen.

Birillo grabbed his penis and slowly penetrated Roberta, making her sigh. He held her firmly by the shoulders and with vigorous strokes of his hips he made her move like a twig in the wind. I could see the man's muscles tense, swell to maintain that precarious balance and pump against the woman. Roberta moaned, she felt that huge member filling her completely and I saw her hands contracting against the edges of the bed to avoid slipping. The woman screamed!

"Fuck me... yes, that's it... give it to me, don't stop..." and then suddenly an animalistic scream came from her throat. She was voicing her own orgasm, her face contorted into a grimace of pleasure and lust that I had never seen before. The controlled, arrogant woman I had known was completely transformed. Under Birillo's incessant blows, at that moment she would have done anything the man asked of her, as long as he didn't stop. Roberta collapsed exhausted on the couch but Birillo had not finished yet. He turned her on her side and started to take her in a rather uncomfortable but effective position. Roberta found new energy.

I was red in the face and I had to do something. I couldn't just stand by and watch my humours drip onto the chair. I apologised to Tobias and ran to my room, where I kept a vibrator. I had to satisfy myself.

CHAPTER 11

I felt guilty.

Poor Giovanni was in the office taking on all the backlog, while I was spending my days in a small room spying on people and masturbating.

But with what the marchioness would have paid, Giovanni would have received a nice bonus too. By now I was like a couch potato. Tobias had also prepared a real-time schedule of events, which he scrolled through the video and updated punctually. A brief summary of the guests and what they were saying to each other. Obviously only the most relevant things. I looked for Federica and saw her huffing in the kitchen; the chef had prepared lunch and was serving courses. Poor thing.

That evening we were going to take stock of the situation with Giorgio; I couldn't wait to see how the other investigations were progressing.

The guests in the pool were making their way to the lounge at a glacial pace. An overlay gave me the afternoon's event. Priestess Patrizia and a photo session with Rossana, scheduled for three o'clock in the afternoon. I didn't feel like having lunch so I went back to my little room to take a nap.

I returned five minutes before three o'clock. I searched through the frames and finally found her. Patrizia was on her way to Rossana's room. She knocked on the door and entered without waiting for an invitation.

"I'm ready!" she said to the guest who was lying on the bed reading a magazine. Rossana looked around bewildered, as if searching for the best place to start taking pictures.

"We could go to one of the rooms upstairs," said Patrizia, "there no one will disturb us. There's a very large one, and it also has a small terrace facing the back, almost hidden. I've already brought some clothes."

"Gladly," said Rossana grabbing a large bag that contained the equipment. The two of them walked down the corridor. I didn't know which room they had chosen and I had to follow them all the way, changing from one frame to another as if I were in a film studio.

The room was large and sunny. It had a double bed on the left, on which clothes were laid, a walnut wardrobe and an armchair. The bathroom was visible through a door. I could see why Patrizia had chosen that room, there was plenty of space to move around and the armchair near the window was an ideal place to use for a photo session. The shutters were ajar, allowing the afternoon sun to filter through. Rossana was fiddling with her camera and lenses.

Patrizia unbuttoned her blouse but Rossana stopped her: "It's a nice uniform, leave it on; why don't you get in the armchair? The light coming through the shutters is ideal."

The priestess was happy to be guided through the photo session. Rossana moved left and right, shooting without interruption, and the model assumed poses that were provocative to say the least. Sitting on the armchair she spread her legs, ran a finger over her lips, lifted her skirt slightly to show her legs. She undid her blouse, revealing a red lace bra that contrasted with her blue and white outfit. Rossana occasionally approached her to fix a detail, a lock of hair, an over-covered shoulder.

Rossana was transfigured, snapping and giving directions, stopping for a moment to change position and then resuming undaunted.

Patrizia had slowly undressed and was now completely naked. She looked at the camera, smiled, changed pose. She went to position herself on the bed where she assumed more explicit postures. One hand between her legs, crawling with her bottom facing the camera, she even started to touch herself.

Rossana was hot, drops of sweat beading on her forehead. She took off her blouse and started looking for details, close-ups, curves that only she and her camera could see. She climbed onto the bed to take better pictures and, while she was on top of Patrizia, Patrizia wrapped her legs around her.

"Have you ever had yourself photographed?" asked the priestess.

"No, I don't like it very much. I don't know," said Rossana defensively.

"Show me how it's done!" Patrizia grabbed the camera and Rossana's hands with it, pulling it towards her. The two fell over each other with a thunderous laugh. The hostess was lying on top of the priestess and looking intently into her eyes, the camera was the only thing standing between the two. She briefly explained the controls to her and Patrizia began to take pictures of her. Every so often she stopped and removed some of Rossana's clothes before continuing. The two remained naked on the bed, intimate. Occasionally Patrizia would allow herself to caress her new friend's face, a light brushing of breasts before taking a new position to photograph.

She placed the camera on the bed and asked Rossana to stand against the headboard, "No, not from behind. There, that's the way your back is against it. Now extend one leg and leave the other bent. That's it. Close your eyes."

Patrizia put the machine down again and lightly stroked her friend's legs. Rossana let her, biting her lip as she kept her eyes closed. She reached into one of the nearby drawers and picked up a pair of handcuffs. She snapped them around Rossana's wrists securing her to the iron headboard before Rossana could say anything. The guest opened her eyes, but Patrizia's gentle, angelic face told her to keep them closed, to let go. And so she did.

Patrizia bent down and kissed her sex.

Rossana jumped backwards and, gripped by fear, opened her eyes again and asked, "What are you doing!?!"

"Relax," whispered the priestess, "I could tell you're excited, I could feel it."

"Yeah ... but ... I mean, I don't feel like it ..."

"Shhh..." whispered Patrizia, "That's it, that's a good girl, close your eyes. Imagine you're in the middle of nowhere on an island..." and as she spoke to her, the priestess's hands rested on her guest's body again. She caressed her legs, her firm, hard breasts, her flat stomach. Her hair brushed Rossana, almost tickling her; it was like a light breeze that contrasted with those curious fingers. Patrizia went back to kissing her on the sex and this time Rossana let her, without remonstrance or fear. The priestess had her in her power.

I looked around but on the other monitors there was nothing else to observe. Giorgio and Valerio were in the gym sweating like crazy. The other nephew, Paolo, and his partner Martina were in their room dozing.

I put the priestess and her new victim back on the main screen. The good Tobias, who up until then had been busy editing audio and video, had gone to get a coffee and came back in a few moments to spill it on me.

"Hey, watch it!"

"Excuse me. Giorgio hadn't warned me what we were up to. I mean, broadly speaking but that..." he said pointing his finger at the giant screen.

"Yep, a nice little live film! Take a break if you want," I said pointing to the chair at my side. Tobias put his coffee down on the desk and watched.

He stood there in silence, I could tell from a mile away that he wanted to ask, to comment, but something was blocking him.

Tobias.

He was a good-looking guy, if a bit young for me. He kept himself fit by going to the gym, no doubt. From under his tank top sprouted two nice firm pecs. I found myself fantasizing about his abs.

"Tobias, how old are you?" I asked offhandedly and then silently cursed myself for opening my mouth.

"Twenty-four, why?"

"Just to determine if you're old enough to look at such things," I said.

He shrugged. Come on Linnea, leave him alone, I said to myself, but then I was curious to know what kind of dick he had. Maybe Giorgio was taking on all courgette. Maybe it was the elusive Italian salami. What if it had been mozzarella? I would have had to work with him for days to come, maybe I shouldn't have screwed up and avoid the risk of blowing everything up.

Meanwhile the priestess, on the screen, had taken possession of a vibrator and was fucking Rossana. Then she turned her over and took her from behind. She alternated between strokes of the vibrator and expert kisses on the sex of the unfortunate, who was panting and moaning like an obsessive. What a scene! She managed to bring her to the brink of orgasm, interrupted herself and then started again. Rossana was sweating and begging for mercy, "Let me come, please! ... Here, don't stop... Nooo! Don't stop."

When she was cooked just right, Patrizia penetrated her again with the dildo and this time she did not stop. She plunged that object into her partner's sex, the humours were visible on that rubber phallus and glistened in the soft sunlight between the shutters. A blow, then another. And finally Rossana's moan of pleasure, which seemed interminable. Patrizia licked her victim's juices off the dildo and then came underneath. She took her by the thighs and pulled her towards herself. Then she climbed on top of her, positioning her sex against Rossana's mouth. From the moans of approval, I could guess that the host had not backed down and was now doing her part.

A brief glance at Tobias revealed a sinister bulge in his trousers, which the young man was trying to hide by keeping his legs crossed. He didn't look at all like the mozzarella type. I would have investigated further but not that afternoon.

"I'm going to take a shower. Ice cold!" I said.

"I'm coming too! No... I mean... not together, I mean on my own. There you go, freshen up."

"Don't worry Tobias, I understood."

Maybe one of these days we'll take a shower together. Better keep your options open.

CHAPTER 12

That evening, Giorgio and Federica arrived later than usual. "We brought you pizza and beers!" he announced as he entered the studio.

"Hey! There's only one pizza here!" I complained, "where's yours?"

"Dear Linnea, we've been working like mules today, we deserve a nice candlelit dinner and to be waited on hand and foot. As it should be after a busy day!" said Giorgio.

"But..."

"No buts! You just sit here wrapped up in air conditioning while we wreak havoc. And then if someone sneaks out of the villa and sees you at the restaurant? How do you explain that?" he continued.

"But..."

"And then I brought you the latest updates on the investigation. You need sharp, unwearied eyes to sift through the results." And so saying, he placed a stack of papers on my table, rattling the beer bottle, took Federica under his arm and headed for the exit.

Fuck! Fuck! Fuck!

I didn't mind him going out with my best friend,

but being left out, that wrinkled me a little. After all, it was me who'd introduced them. And above all, I didn't feel like eating pizza and beer when I could have been feasting on lobster and scallops.

I started leafing through the file Giorgio had left me. Then I went back to the screen. From the computer that controlled it all, I could choose any piece of film I wanted. I began to search randomly through the last hour of footage. Suddenly Giorgio and Federica appeared, laughing in the distance at the end of a corridor. They were closer than the etiquette allowed and I couldn't hear what they were saying. Giorgio was whispering words, I imagined sweet, in Federica's ear and she was laughing.

God, I had lost them!

Those looks were as clear as day, the two were flirting, there was something in the air. Then Giorgio kissed her.

The thing that got on my nerves was that it wasn't a passionate kiss, the kind that says, 'I want to fuck you now, immediately, at this very moment!' No, that was a sensual kiss, saying, 'I like you, I want to get to know you better'.

If Giorgio and Federica also fell into the trap of becoming a couple I had only one option. Die alone and a spinster!

Did I have to say it? Did I have to admit it with a

nice 'I'm happy for them'? Probably yes, but at that moment the only thought that was going through my mind was murder. I was going to kill that pizza and then drown it in beer, just to be on the safe side.

I went back to looking at the files. The first two were about Paolo and his wife Martina, who up until then had thought it best to keep her legs closed. Bridge club, mortgage, car repayments, boat holidays, home contents insurance and... Wait a minute! That mortgage payment was exorbitant. With his job for a multinational food company, he couldn't afford boat trips, a car like that. His wife, as far as we could tell, didn't make pots of money. She was a freelance writer, not attached to any major publishing house. She certainly wasn't making much. The two of them were living beyond their means; it wouldn't have taken much to push them into the abyss of poverty. They had a motive to murder the old woman, and the still waters...

I moved on to Rossana.

A modest life, several entries in photo contests, none won, a job as a pharmacist but she didn't own the pharmacy. If she had money, she didn't show it by the monotonous life she led. It was not a good motive but I suspended judgement.

A different story about Giulia and Sergio. From

the analysis carried out, it appeared that Sergio had two lovers. One lived in Naples, where he often went for work, and the other was his secretary. I made a toast to originality with the last sip of beer. The good Giulia instead had a passion for masochism. Parties, films I already knew about and a job as a lawyer. Shit, I should have reported her to the Order. They let everyone practice these days. She dealt with divorces and cases like that, she wasn't going to starve but she didn't seem to be making a fortune either. On the contrary, Sergio was very good at spending his fortune. According to his records, he was a heavy gambler, playing poker frequently and often losing. The casinos did not give him any credit despite the fact that he boasted left and right of a title of marquis, which did not yet belong to his wife. In a republic, you don't get anywhere with just the name Marquis on your business cards.

The only ones who seemed to be doing well were Roberta and her husband Valerio. They had bought a house in Lübeck, were living in the centre of Milan, had no debts, and an unspecified number of investments had raised their bank accounts. The two talked of nothing but money. Or rather Roberta did, Valerio agreed. The emails from Roberta's private computer showed a chilling scene. The woman was greedy for money, she controlled every single transaction of her husband and gave him unbelievable tirades when he spent more than necessary. They had bought flats and resold them at a profit. They had invested in a car dealership and sold it before the car market collapsed. The Excel spreadsheets that Giorgio's co-workers had seized showed large investments in shares, some in start-ups. Maybe she was using her position at the bank to do a bit of insider trading. While money might not be a motive, the obsession that drove her gave rise to doubts. Could it be that she also wanted the old woman's fortune? With one-sixth of seven hundred million, she could have created an empire.

While for one reason or another anyone in this group could have been involved in the marchioness's accident, the data I had in my hands still did not justify murder. It was mostly conjecture.

The only one who seemed unproblematic was Tiziano, the one who had arrived and left on a motorbike. He was the owner of a racing bicycle factory, had received awards and recognition for his use of technologically advanced materials, and had even been in the newspaper for an innovative, lightweight, folding bike. He was engaged and had a child and seemed to live a happy life. No debts, no nothing.

I went to sleep without waiting for Federica and Giorgio to return.

CHAPTER 13

The next day passed without a hitch but also without anything noteworthy. I was shitting myself. If we hadn't managed to find the culprit among the grandchildren, then we would have been left with few options in our hands. The fact was that the marchioness was old and well-liked. Even if she had had enemies, many would have died of natural causes by now, given the lady's age. Giorgio's boys had looked into her possessions, into potential conflicts in her portfolio, but the investigation was revealing nothing.

Had it all been a misunderstanding? That the marchioness's accident was just a trivial driving error, despite her swearing to the contrary?

We were spending a lot of money on that surveillance; the rent for the villa where I was staying with Tobias was significant. I didn't know if Patrizia and Birillo were being paid in any way, but it seemed likely that they were. Giorgio's bill was going to be huge and so was mine.

Fuck! I hated going home empty-handed.

Another day went by and finally the moods

woke up. Or rather, the frets.

A brief glimpse of the cameras revealed Valerio and Paolo doing exercises in the gym. The two gave the impression that they knew each other, although I had sworn otherwise, both from the first impression I had made and from Giorgio's initial reports.

In a corridor downstairs Roberta was dragging Giulia by the arm, like a teacher who has caught a naughty student red-handed. They wandered around the villa until they found Birillo.

"This is the little bitch I told you about," Roberta said.

Birillo looked around, as if to avoid being surprised by a non-existent master, and then, conspiratorially said, "Follow me."

Birillo led the way and guided them to the upper floors, but not before stopping to take a leather bag from a small room.

I started fiddling with the controls so as not to lose them. They had chosen the farthest room, diametrically opposite the pool and the gym.

"Get undressed!" ordered Roberta.

Poor Giulia obeyed and slowly took off her blouse and trousers, remaining only in her underwear.

"Take that off too!"

The slave, without making any complaints, did as ordered, remaining completely naked in front of the two. It was at that point that Birillo extracted several jute ropes from his bag, some very long. He took Giulia by the shoulders and spun her around, then pushed her down until she was on her knees.

"Among the various Kinbaku that can be used," Birillo explained, "this is the technique called Koutou ushiro te shibari." He took one of the ropes and began to tie Giulia up. Roberta looked admiringly at the man's hands as he worked with the laces. The result was splendid. Giulia had both arms tied behind her back. Her forearms were parallel and surrounded by ropes at the wrists. Jute was then wrapped around her arms and secured behind her back. The result resembled the letter T. The rope was passed several times around one arm, then around Guilia's torso and then around the other arm. This created the upper part of the letter T. Knots and twists were skilfully made. Next, the rope had secured the forearms, forming the shaft of the letter.

"This technique allows you to work on the subject on the ground, or if you prefer, to suspend it," Birillo explained.

Roberta admired his work, following the strings

with a finger. She caressed Giulia's body, tested the ligatures, confirming to herself that they were securely fastened, and then gave the prisoner a tug. "Good, very good!" she said, "Sounds complicated."

"With a little practice you can master it," said Birillo.

Roberta licked her lips; she was getting excited at the new possibilities these techniques were promising her. What she had done so far to her cousin was amateur practice, here it was going on another level.

"Show me some more!" she said.

Birillo untied the woman, took a much longer rope and got busy. I couldn't follow his movements, Birillo was going too fast, but slowly shapes were emerging from Giulia's body. The result was another amazing design, like a spider's web woven on the woman's back, and secured to her arms, shoulders and wrists. The web had three concentric octagons and was a work of art. "This is a variation of the Kikkou shibari technique," said Birillo, "In fact, a more complicated version of the previous one."

"Too difficult," Roberta murmured, "can you show me something I can do too?"

"Sure. These techniques require study and dedication, but they are very effective."

As Birillo untied the woman I lingered over the other monitors. Valerio and Paolo had finished their exercises and were in the shower. Wait a moment! I thought. I put them on the main screen and there was no doubt. The two of them were showing a nice erection in progress and were looking at each other. Paolo, who seemed to be the most enterprising, reached out a hand and grabbed Valerio's penis. He pulled it to himself and lathered it up very carefully.

"Given the choice, I would have looked at the others," Tobias said from behind.

"HOLY CHRIST! Is that any way to sneak up on someone? Sit down and be quiet!" I said, pointing to the chair on my right. Tobias did not hesitate.

I put Birillo and company on the screen. He had finished the job and was now showing Roberta another technique. This one seemed less complex but still interesting. Ropes were wrapped around Giulia's torso, above and below her breasts. A loop of rope passed around her neck and her arms were tied behind her back. At that point Birillo tied the woman's legs in such a way as to leave them open. Her knees were close to her torso. From the way she was tied she looked ready for a missionary, but she could not have made any movements.

Again Roberta admired the work by following

the contours of the ropes. She then dwelled on Giulia's sex, finding it wet.

"Can you fuck her, with all those ties?" asked Roberta.

"Of course," said Birillo.

"Then fuck her!"

The man didn't hesitate, he pulled down his trousers and in a moment he had an erection. He pulled Giulia towards him using the ropes and in a moment he was inside her, making her moan.

Roberta stood on a small armchair, lifted her skirt and began to masturbate in front of the two of them.

"I need a cold shower!" I said to Tobias. Fuck, I'd never washed so much in my life.

CHAPTER 14

The whispers and murmurs began the next day in the late afternoon.

The leader was Roberta. She walked around talking under her breath first to one cousin then to the other.

"Is there no way to hear what they're saying to each other?" I asked Tobias in frustration.

"Hardly. They're really whispering and the microphones don't pick up well. I'll have to run the audio through the equalizer, put some filters on..."

"Do it! Don't waste time!" I commanded him.

The marchioness was arriving that evening and the last thing I wanted was to put her in danger. That group seemed to know each other well, despite the files telling the contrary.

Tobias worked magic and eventually managed to extract clips of audio.

"But there are risks! We're all in the villa, they'll suspect us for sure," said Paolo.

"Suspicion is one thing, evidence is another," Roberta replied. "It's true, we're all in the villa, but she's old. A stroke could happen to anyone."

Then there was a croaking of indistinct voices.

The only word that could be heard was 'tonight' followed by other background noises, the wind and indistinct murmurs.

"...together...if we stick together there will be no problems...before she sign the will!"

That was enough for me. I left the villa in a hurry and headed towards Milan. Maybe I still had time to stop the marchioness.

I called countess Casati on the phone but got no answer. "Countess, it's Linnea, call me immediately as soon as you get this message! This is a matter of the utmost urgency!"

I called Giorgio. No answer. I called Federica. No answer! Shit, those two were surely fucking like hedgehogs, forgetting why we were at the villa.

The clinic! I had to call the clinic!

Looking for a phone number while driving on the highway at a hundred and eighty kilometres per hour is not an easy task. Then you have to waste time with receptionists who don't have the word 'urgent' in their vocabulary. In the end, after many attempts, I reached a nurse who informed me that the marchioness had left the clinic.

Shit! I was already in Binasco. I took the exit and re-entered the A7 from the opposite side. Come on, Linnea, you can do it, I told myself.

If I'd come out unscathed, I would have left the

law for a career in politics. *The Party for the abolition of speed limits* I would have called it, or *get out of the fucking lane.*

The last few kilometres to Portofino were done in no time at all, and a job as a rally driver was not to be missed.

I parked outside the villa when it was already pitch dark. I knew where they were going to put the marchioness, we'd discussed it to death, but if I'd run into the villa like a madwoman I would have warned them. Maybe it was the right thing to do. What if they were already in the old woman's room?

I looked around. There was a hundred-year-old wisteria climbing the wall of the villa, I would use that!

I took off my shoes and started to climb. The window was luckily ajar and I crawled into the room like a cat. It was pitch black, I couldn't see a damn thing. I huddled in a corner under the window, thinking about what to do while my eyes adjusted to the darkness. I could hear the old woman breathing deeply, not far from me. Footsteps in the corridor. There they were! They were coming.

Then I panicked.

What could I do? I wasn't armed, at most I could have thrown mascara at them. Maybe they would have given up if they found me in the room. Or maybe they would have killed me too!

I cursed Giorgio and his frenzy, that asshole couldn't keep that cock in his trousers if he was paid for it.

The handle moved and the door opened. I could see shadows in the corridor; fucking everyone was there, not just Roberta!

Screaming! I should have screamed at the top of my lungs, someone would have heard, maybe Birillo. I took a breath, I was ready.

The light came on and Giorgio, with a gun in his hand shouted "Stop everyone!"

He had come out from behind a cupboard in the room. The guests froze, like rabbits caught in the headlights of a car.

"Put that syringe down! Put it down on the table without making a fuss."

Roberta placed the syringe containing green liquid on the small table next to it and raised her hands.

"Don't do anything stupid and everything will be fine. The police will be here any minute!"

Paolo did not obey Giorgio's peremptory order and lunged at him. He didn't have time to reach him when a BANG sounded in the room, making my ears ring. Paolo fell to the ground; a red stain was forming on his chest.

"Does anyone want to end up like him?" asked Giorgio.

Nobody moved. Giorgio picked up the walkie-talkie.

"How much longer?"

From the other side a voice croaked, "They should already be there, I can see the cars coming into the villa."

It was Tobias.

I peeked out the window and saw the blue flashing lights, which made me finally relax. My gaze fell on the marchioness's bed. A pile of pillows stood in its place, they had moved her somewhere else. The police arrived and handcuffed everyone in the room while Giorgio put his gun away. "Don't forget the syringe!" he said. "My colleague is on his way with all the tapes and intercepts."

My legs were shaking and I needed something strong. Giorgio noticed and accompanied me down the stairs.

"What did you think you were going to do in that room, scratching them with your nails?" asked Giorgio.

"I don't know. I was only thinking of defending the marchioness."

I slumped down in an armchair and Giorgio brought me a glass of brandy. A few minutes later we were joined by Federica, Birillo, Countess Casati and the priestess.

"And the marchioness?"

"She stayed at the clinic. We used one of my collaborators, dressed and made up as needed, as a stand-in."

"And you didn't tell me a damn thing? Christ, I set the speed record on the Milan-Genoa highway. And why didn't you answer your phone?"

"I was busy making the trap work."

"That was a nice gesture of yours," the countess told me. I took a sip and looked around; everyone was smiling and Giorgio and Federica were holding hands.

"Tiziano," the countess continued, "was above suspicion. He is now at the clinic with the marchioness. They have a lot of explaining to do, but I think everything will be fine."

I had risked my neck for nothing, Giorgio and my best friend had got together and I felt empty inside. At least I'd get a decent fee.

CHAPTER 15

There were a lot of things still to sort out, after the drama of the night before. The police came and went but they wanted statements, the tapes and all sorts of paperwork was waiting for me for the days to come. Not that I was going to complain, I was paid enough to sort out all the outcomes of the criminal investigation that, for sure, was going to happen after the events that had taken place. So were the Italian police, they didn't like to be handed over all the evidence of a crime and say "thank you very much". They would have wanted to review everything, taking new statements, doing their own part of form-filling. Bureaucracy was our second nature, we liked to give our contribution to the Amazon deforestation.

But all that will have to wait; it would have taken the police weeks to go through all the documentation. That morning I took the executive decision to be miserable under the hot sun of *Liguria*. It must have been three in the morning when we reached our beds and I didn't sleep a bit. Maybe it was the adrenaline or maybe it was the sense of disappointment that had taken me over in the past few days. I couldn't tell.

The Countess reached me by the pool after about an hour or so, just when I was going to doze off.

"Linnea! Here you are, I searched the whole villa looking for you."

"Yeah, I thought I needed a bit of peace and quiet after last night's fracas." I looked at her through my sunglasses. She was fresh as a daisy.

"You don't seem too happy, which is strange, as this whole *operation* of yours has been an outstanding success. I have to apologise to you if I had to push you, but you have helped save a life. God knows what would have happened to Gemma without you. By the way, she sends her regards and her gratitude."

I nodded. I wasn't in the mood for having a chat. I mulled over the events of the past year and nothing had really changed in my life. It was almost as if everything happened to everybody else except me. The Countess and Dionisiya, Giorgio and Federica. And what about me? Was I going to end up like Giovanni, with more money than I needed and the only satisfaction in my life coming from my work? Was I really going to end up like my associate, alone with a bunch of folders for companions for my Saturday's nights? I had fucked up; I knew it. As much as I tried to convince myself that I had a life that fulfilled me, deep inside I knew it was just a lie. I worked hard because the alternative would be to look inside and see the vast emptiness that my life was. All the adventures, the work, the flirting were bandages and band-aids to cover what I was too scared to face. People would have laughed at me if I said out loud I was scared shitless, they would not take me seriously. It would be something unheard of for me, something inconceivable. But that was the hard truth.

"...I would say you take the week off and maybe stay here at the villa. At least until Sunday, what do you think Linnea?"

I was so engrossed in being miserable that I missed pretty much everything the Countess was telling me. But a week off, where I could drown my sorrow in alcohol, perhaps was not the worst scenario. The alternative was to go back to Milan and work. No, thank you.

"If it is not too much of an imposition, I'd love that," I muttered.

"Good. Please do expense your staying here to Gemma, she said so very vigorously, and then Saturday night there is a surprise for you at the restaurant *Puny.*"

"A surprise?"

"Indeed. If you miss it, I will be really upset," she

added.

"I won't. Thank you, Countess."

I sat there looking at the empty space in front of me. It was a long time since I had had a surprise. People didn't really surprise me anymore; most of the time they disappointed me, but this was a gift; coming from her it would have been something expensive I imagined. I missed another couple of sentences until I realised she was still talking to me.

"… and you were right, that investigator of yours is really a talent," she winked at me and stood up from the sun chair. I thanked her and got lost in my thoughts. Again.

The next few days passed uneventful; I didn't even get drunk as I planned to. Well, a bit but not too much.

I walked down from the villa to the lovely main square in Portofino and turned toward the restaurant. I was planning to murder a couple of lobsters and vaporize as many bottles of wine I could get my hands on when I had to stop in my step, breathless.

In front of me, twenty meters far away and sitting at one of the tables on the seafront was Patricia, smiling and waving at me.

"What the heck…" I ran towards her as fast as I

could without losing my dignity and threw my arm around her. I kissed her and then I did it again, before I ran out of breath. "How is this possible… your visa…"

"Surprise!"

It was a surprise indeed. How in hell had the Countess managed to have pulled a trick like this out of the hat?

"Your visa…"

"Sit down and take a breath, I'll explain everything," she said.

I did as I was told, eager to know more.

"Fancy a glass of wine?" she asked.

"Sure, why not. Let's make it two. As long as you explain by what kind of magic you happen to be here. Tell me, you didn't come here illegally, did you?"

"Not at all. At the beginning I thought it was a scam or a bad joke. I've been tracked down by a private investigator. It was all hush hush and they made me swear not to tell you anything over the phone. Bottom line, this lady, Ms Casati, had a friend, or a friend of a friend, that needed an actress here in Italy. This guy put together a theatre where they play in English for children. A way of learning the language in a fun way."

"That sounds amazing…"

"I'm not finished yet; all this comes with a work

visa; no more six months at a time. It seemed the only reasonable option to be together again. Somehow, I could not see you moving to Nebraska; not many chances for you to practice Italian law in the Mid-West."

I could not see myself there either, but that was not the point. Practicing law was a choice and I was good at it, but it was a choice. Moving to another country would have also been a choice, and it would have been an easy decision if I knew who I was and was in love. The fact was that I had lied to myself, I was chasing dreams, I was trying to be the cool, open minded, liberated gal; not afraid to express her sexuality to the entire world. I was kidding myself and Patricia forced me to have a deep look inside of me. All of the adventures I had were there to put a lid on something that, perhaps, I always knew. I was a lesbian. All the rest was a highly elaborated cover up. I just needed the right person to open up with. After all, I didn't need to ask the Countess about her motivations to become a lesbian. I had my own.

And then I start crying. A heavy weight was suddenly removed from my chest and I could not stop sobbing like a baby.

"Linnea, what's going on..." she asked, the doubt was clear in her expression. She had decided for the both of us a decision that I might have never been able to make alone.

"I'm ok, really. I'm so happy you are here. Patricia," I sobbed, "I love you."

"I love you too. Oh my gosh, you scared the bejesus out of me."

"Really, it is all good. I better sort myself out."

And then she told me how everybody chipped in. Not only Giorgio and the Countess. Giovanni helped too, sorting through my items in the office and finding Patricia's address. Federica helped in conveying Ms Casati's wishes into common language. Apparently, everybody else knew exactly what I needed, except me.

That night we made love as if it was the first time for me. In a sense it was. And I knew I didn't need any more adventures in my life. The biggest one had just started.

*****The End*****

Printed in Great Britain
by Amazon